A TIME FOR TENDERNESS

Other Books by the Same Author

FANCY FREE
ACCENT ON APRIL
THE SCARLET SAIL
STARS IN HER EYES
ANGEL ON SKIS
THE BOY NEXT DOOR
PASSPORT TO ROMANCE

Published by William Morrow and Company

A TOUCH OF MAGIC
6 ON EASY STREET
LOVE, LAURIE
LASSO YOUR HEART
TWO'S COMPANY
SPRING COMES RIDING
PAINTBOX SUMMER
A GIRL CAN DREAM
SPURS FOR SUZANNA
GOING ON SIXTEEN
THE BLACK SPANIEL MYSTERY
PUPPY STAKES

Published by The Westminster Press

A Time
for Tenderness

by

BETTY CAVANNA

WILLIAM MORROW AND COMPANY

NEW YORK

1962

ACKNOWLEDGMENTS

For much in this book I am indebted to my mother, Emily Allen Cavanna, who led me to consider character rather than color a test of worth, to Marlene dos Santos, an intelligent young Carioca, with whom I was able to discuss frankly the Brazilian scene, to Katya Overhage, a helpful critic and friend, and to my editor, Connie Epstein, who encouraged and guided me.

A TIME FOR TENDERNESS

"A little fun, to match the sorrow
Of each day's growing. . . ."
George du Maurier

Chapter 1

"Margaret Cullen Jamison," wrote Peggy on the card of admission to the Escola Americana. She sat at a table in the school office, her head bent in concentration, her copper-colored hair glinting like a new penny in the sun that streamed through the open window.

Date—"August 7." Age—"16," wrote Peggy. Then she checked off the subjects the headmaster had explained she would be expected to take: Geometry, Biology, Speech, English, French, Portuguese.

Home address? requested the card, and from force of habit she almost wrote, "22 Country Club Drive, Charlotte, North Carolina." Then she remembered, with some difficulty, the number of the apartment house on Avenida Atlântica, which was the address the school would expect. But it wasn't home, Peggy thought with a wave of nostalgia. It never would be. Nor would this school ever take the place of Country Day.

"Transplanting is seldom easy," her father had said, in the way adults have of making metaphors. "The

11

roots always suffer a shock, but then usually a plant blooms better than ever in new earth, and in a new pot."

The American School in Rio was going to be a pretty big flowerpot, Peggy recognized wryly. Eight hundred pupils from thirty different countries besides Brazil were going to be pounding around these halls.

Of course, Peggy assured herself with sudden courage, just being here is bound to be exciting. She remembered the envy of her friends when she had announced that she was going to live for a year or more in South America.

"Lucky you!" Laurette King had breathed. "Think of the beaches! And I understand Brazilian boys are super. Marvelous dancers and terribly interested in blondes."

"I'm not a blonde, I'm a redhead," Peggy had reminded her, but Laurette had merely shrugged. "You're close enough."

It was true, Peggy realized after only three days in Rio, that her hair attracted attention. People turned to glance at her a second time, not rudely, but curiously, as though she were a rare or remarkable bird. At first it had embarrassed her, but gradually it was beginning to amuse her, because she could see that their attention was meant as a compliment.

The first of these interested glances had come from the white-coated customs man at the airport on the night of the Jamisons' arrival. He had smiled at Peggy warmly and chalked pass marks on her suitcases without even asking her to open them.

"You must look more innocent than I'd realized," her mother had teased in an undertone, as she struggled with the zippers on her own overcrowded bags.

Peggy's first glimpse of Rio had been from the air, as the plane pushed down through twilit clouds. A bay, fringed by crescent beaches; deep-purple mountains; and then the dun-colored rush of the airstrip under the jet's lowered wheels.

Later, in a high-hipped, old-fashioned taxi, the Jamisons had rattled along a strange dark road lined with warehouses. Beyond these, Peggy realized vaguely, lay miles of docks facing Guanabara Bay. Her shoulders twitched involuntarily, and her mother, sitting beside her in a trim gray traveling suit, asked, "Cold, dear?"

Peggy shook her head, rejecting the flutter of apprehension that had traced its way down her spine. How could she explain that it was just excitement, the same sort of mixed alarm and anticipation that flooded her now as she sat filling out the form in the registrar's office.

She remembered her mother's next remark, the eagerness in her voice as the cab rounded a bend into a marine drive, pricked by thousands of lights. "Oh, look, Charles! This must be the Golden Necklace they talk about."

Peggy's father had nodded in gratification at such enthusiasm and leaned forward to tap his eight-year-old son on the shoulder, concerned that, because he was sharing the front seat with the driver, he might miss something. "Isn't this pretty fabulous, Tobey?"

Tobey had inclined his head in mild approval, and Peggy sympathized with his hesitation about committing himself. How could a person decide, at first encounter, what a city was like?

"Wait 'til you see Rio in the daylight!" her father was urging. "It's impossible to describe the color in the mountains and sea and sky."

"I think this is going to be fun!" Virginia Jamison burst forth. She was leaning forward between her husband and her daughter, turning her head from side to side as though she was afraid a detail might escape her glance.

Peggy had been swept by another shiver of trepidation. Fun, for her, was inextricably entangled with her special crowd, with the club swimming pool, with the debuts planned for fall, and with Jim Barton, who had promised to write once a week.

Sitting very still, Peggy had kept staring out the window as though mesmerized by the lights that curved along the bay, but actually she was facing afresh the reality of moving to Brazil. The crowd would break up, as more and more of the girls went away to school, Laurette would come out at a party Peggy couldn't attend, and Jim was not a lad to moon about a bird in the bush—particularly a South American bush. There was no use dodging the issue. Nothing, when she returned home, would be the same.

The highway had ducked into a long tiled tunnel,

and the taxi rattled through to the far side, turning left, then right, to Copacabana Beach. "Can we go swimming tomorrow?" asked Tobey, bouncing up and down in excitement at first sight of the ocean. "Tomorrow morning, first thing?" This proved that homesickness had never crossed his mind. Then, without waiting for an answer, he added, "Hey! Skyscrapers. Just like New York."

"Not quite that tall," corrected his father. "But tall enough. You see, the mountains keep Rio from growing out, so it has to grow up."

The rest of the taxi ride Peggy could recall only as a blur of whizzing lights curving along the sea. Then the driver had pulled into the crescent-shaped drive of a perpendicular building with a glass-faced lobby, and the family had crowded into an elevator with a jumble of luggage, raincoats, cameras, and flight bags, which pinioned Peggy on all sides.

The apartment her father had rented on a previous trip looked out on the beach from the fifth floor. It was unexpectedly spacious, and a breeze bellied the sheer white curtains like sails on a ship. To Peggy, this made the place seem indescribably foreign, and from then on the billowing white curtains spelled Rio to her, quite as much as the bird kites on the beach, the serpentine mosaic pavements, and the statue of Christ on the mountainside.

The next two days had passed in a haze of new impressions impossible to sort out, and even this morning, filling out the card in the school office, Peggy felt

as insubstantial as a character in a dream. The table at
which she sat, sturdy and scarred though it appeared,
might decide to float away, and the students hurrying
through the hall might develop wings and drift along
a few inches off the floor.

"Almost finished, Margaret?" The headmaster's en-
couraging voice aroused her, although she was unaccustomed to being addressed by her full name.

"Yes, sir—I think so, sir." The softness of Peggy's
Southern accent made her seem immeasurably feminine and appealing.

The headmaster hesitated, smiling down into Peggy's
gray-blue eyes, and said, almost anxiously, "I do hope
you enjoy it here. You'll find a very catholic group of
students."

"Catholic?"

Mr. Hartman laughed, with a return to his usual
heartiness. "Of course most Brazilians *are* Roman
Catholics, but I mean the word in its broader sense.
You'll find a great many different creeds, nationalities,
and colors—young people from all over the world."

"I think that should be very interesting," said Peggy
politely, although she quaked inwardly. In Charlotte
a foreigner was considered "different" and accepted
warily, if at all.

The headmaster moved on into his private office and
Peggy picked up the admission card and pushed back
her chair, wondering what she was expected to do
next. "Just wait here a few minutes," the secretary sug-

gested, "and I'll have one of the students take you on a tour of the classrooms and library and—"

A tall rangy girl with very curly brown hair cropped almost as short as a boy's hesitated in the doorway, and the secretary broke off and called, "Becky! Are you busy? This is Margaret Jamison, who's coming to school here. Somebody should show her around."

Becky hesitated briefly, glancing over her shoulder as though in hope of deliverance, then bowed to her fate and smiled pleasantly. "I've got a committee meeting in just about ten minutes," she said to Peggy. "I hope you can walk fast!"

Peggy felt a small shock of dismay. It was the first time she had ever been a "new girl," an outsider. "I don't want to be a bother," she murmured, as she followed Becky out into the hall. She had a peculiar feeling she had lived through this scene before. In an instant of total recall she realized that the roles had been reversed. *She* had been the one detailed to show a stranger around Country Day, and the girl—a Mary Lou Somebody, whose face was now forgotten—had made the same remark.

"Oh, it's no bother," Becky was saying airily, as she hurried down a corridor. "This is the cafeteria—through these doors. This is the teachers' lunchroom." She led the way to a second floor, and then a third. "This is the chem lab. These are just classrooms. Incidentally, I'm from Indiana. You're from the South, aren't you? Where?"

"North Carolina," Peggy told her, descriptively dropping the "*r.*"

"Oh. Is your father with the State Department?"

Peggy shook her head. "My father's company is opening a branch office down here. He's doing the organization work." She took her turn at a question. "Have you been here long?"

"Two years," Becky said. "What grade will you be in?"

"Tenth," Peggy told her.

The other girl's eyes sparkled with a touch more interest. "I'm a sophomore too. We'll probably be in most of the same classes. D'you know any Portuguese?"

Peggy shook her head. "Not a bit. French is bad enough, but Portuguese scares me to death."

Becky shrugged, as though this remark had no significance. "You pick it up," she said. "After a few months you'll get along fine."

Peggy was dubious, but she didn't argue the point. Instead she concentrated on trying to look more self-assured than she felt. Becky showed her some more classrooms and a top-floor library, then stopped by a vending machine and felt in the pocket of her blouse for some coins. "How about a *guaraná?*" she asked.

"A what?"

Becky grinned. "You *must* be new here! It's a Brazilian drink, sort of like a Coke," she explained, as she opened a bottle of caramel-colored liquid and handed it to her companion. "Try it. It's good."

Conditioned by her mother's advice to be cautious concerning native foods, Peggy regarded the bottle at arm's length, as though it might bite her if she put it to her lips. Becky stopped drinking to laugh again. "Don't worry. You won't get lockjaw or typhoid or even *tourista*. Cross my heart. It's quite safe."

Peggy laughed, unaware that her laughter had an infectious quality that made two passing students turn to glance at her. "You must think I'm an awful dope, but it's all so *strange!*" she murmured. Raising the bottle, she took a tentative sip, and her eyes widened. "It *is* good," she admitted, with obvious surprise.

Suddenly everything became easy. Instead of making conversational forays, the girls began to talk together like old campaigners, each cognizant of the line of march. "The first few days are awful," Becky remembered. "I felt absolutely grim about everything. But honestly this won't last. You'll get to know people much faster than back in the States, because everybody—but everybody!—has been new here pretty recently. So you make friends easier somehow. You'll see."

Peggy gulped, her throat tight with appreciation. "You give me courage," she confessed.

"Look," Becky proposed, in an access of good will. "I've got to run now, but meet me for lunch. I'll introduce you to some of the kids in our class."

This promise armored Peggy for the morning. She sat through assembly and three forty-five minute classes, outwardly calm, but with her heart still doing flutter kicks. English wasn't too bad; the class was starting where she had left off at Country Day. Geometry was difficult, as could be expected. But French was pure poison; it seemed to Peggy that all the girls —even the pretty ones—could jabber like a flock of educated magpies. She felt certain she'd never catch up.

Not a moment too soon came the break for lunch, and along with about half of the two hundred students from the high-school classes, Peggy moved along a hall, walled with green glass mosaic, toward the cafeteria.

Surrounded by strangers, she felt like a fragment of driftwood rushed along by a torrent. Everyone seemed to be calling greetings, making engagements, exchanging gossip, or indulging in nonsense repartee. While they looked around her, above her, and beyond her as though she were invisible, Peggy needed the courage she had claimed. It's always difficult for a new girl, she told herself, and remembered guiltily that last year she had never given a second thought to the new girls at Country Day.

Standing on tiptoe, peering over the shoulders of the boys and girls in front of her, Peggy looked anxiously but unsuccessfully for Becky's curly head. Panic swept her at the thought of carrying a laden tray to a table occupied by strangers. She'd rather starve!

At the very point of ducking out of the line now approaching the long cafeteria counter, Peggy felt a light tap on her arm. She turned to find a tray, with the

usual complement of knife, fork, and spoon, being offered to her. *"Por favor,"* said a masculine voice.

The hand holding the tray was firm-wristed. A fraction of an inch of white cuff was visible below the
sleeve of an olive-green jacket. Following the sleeve
upward, Peggy encountered a slender tanned neck, a
boyish chin, a broad mouth, and dark eyes which
danced with mischief.

"Thank you very much," she murmured, aware that
she was flushing, and also aware that the boy behind
her was handsome, in a Latin sort of way. His hair
was the color of bitter chocolate, with a shine to it, his
nose was patrician and straight, his eyes had blue-
white pupils, and he looked relaxed and mildly amused.

Yet he didn't introduce himself or embark on a conversation. He was right behind Peggy as she filled her
tray. Because of his presence, she selected a salad
rather than the hamburger she would have preferred.
He didn't speak to her again, in spite of the fact that
she turned and glanced back at him as she approached
the cashier.

Alone, Peggy moved out into the crowded sea of
tables. Then, to her relief, she caught sight of a raised
hand, beckoning from the far corner of the room. Below it was a recognizable cropped head, and as Becky
stood up with a welcoming smile, Peggy steered a
course through the chattering crowd of students, holding her tray up out of harm's way.

"Hi there. We saved a place for you." Becky managed to be both casual and cordial. "This is Linda

Paul," she said, indicating a plump rosy-cheeked girl with sandy hair. "Ann Tjian." Peggy nodded to a slender, olive-skinned Chinese, with slanting eyes and straight black bangs. "Cleonice Andrade. Cleo for short."

Cleo, who was romantic-looking in the sort of way Peggy associated with flamenco dancing and a rose behind one ear, moved her chair closer to Linda's. "Maybe you can squeeze in here," she invited politely, but without special enthusiasm.

Actually, the table had been intended for four, so Peggy especially appreciated Becky's arrangements to make room for her. She acknowledged the introductions with a smile intended to be winning, and glanced gratefully at the chair, which had been reserved by the simple method of piling it high with books.

Becky and the Chinese girl, called by the curiously English name of Ann, removed these and stacked them in the corner, while Peggy unloaded her tray and sat down. She was completely aware that Becky's friends were sizing her up, that although their glances were deliberately uncurious they were conscious of her clothes, of her Carolina accent, of her winter-pale skin, and of the simple North American manner in which she was wearing her hair.

Peggy, in turn, was deciding that Linda looked too dumpy to be interesting, that the girl with the name like Chan was almost frighteningly foreign, that Cleo must be Portuguese and was probably considered a knockout by the boys.

It was Cleo who turned to the new girl now, and said on a note of amusement, "I saw you talking to Dom Carlos over in the line."

"To whom?" Peggy felt that her ears must be playing tricks.

From across the table Becky laughed. "That's just a nickname for Carlos Almeida."

"Because he's so good looking," added Linda, with no attempt to conceal her admiration. "He's the living picture of a Portuguese grandee."

"Carlos is what you'd call Cleo's 'kissin' cousin,' " put in Becky impishly.

"He's a *very distant* relative," admitted Cleo lazily, and Peggy, pretending to address her attention to the salad, for which she wasn't in the least hungry, knew quite well that she was being warned to keep hands off.

She looked up innocently, although inwardly delighted that this beautiful creature should consider her sufficiently attractive to be a threat. "You mean the boy who took pity on me and handed me a tray? I scarcely noticed him," she fibbed.

Cleo raised a meticulously arched eyebrow, but Becky interceded and cried, "Let the poor girl get her breath before you give her a run-down on the male personnel. This is her maiden voyage, remember?" She looked at Peggy sympathetically.

Along with everyone else, Peggy laughed. "In one way," she said, in genuine amusement, "I guess Rio's not much different from Charlotte. No matter where you are, boys have a way of coming first."

Chapter 2

Although far from subtle or clever, the amiable candor of this remark ingratiated Peggy to the luncheon-table group, and from then on she found it easy to be natural, and natural to be accepted. With Southern good breeding, she kept her voice calm, her smile bright, and her eyes interested as she was introduced to more and more of her classmates. By the end of the afternoon she had a nodding acquaintance with a dozen or more girls and boys, although it was still difficult to sort out names and faces.

Riding back to the apartment on the bus, which traveled along the Avenida Atlântica, Peggy felt exhausted but almost elated. The hurdles ahead were certainly no higher than the one behind.

It was wonderful to be released from that first miserable stage fright. In contrast to the morning, when she had ridden to school in a taxi beside her mother, entirely oblivious to the passing scene, Peggy began to look with interest at this city in which she would spend the next year.

The profile of Copacabana Beach, turned toward the sea, was sleek and streamlined, a sequence of hotels and apartment houses, pointed like square white pencils into the blue box of the sky. On the right of the bus a sidewalk of black and white mosaic tiles curved along the broad beach. A few boys were playing volley ball and an occasional bather breasted the surf, but by this time in the afternoon the sun had dropped behind the mountains, and the sands were almost deserted. A stream of cars was winding out of town, and sidewalk cafés were beginning to fill with people, sipping coffee or *apéritifs*. To Peggy, who before this trip had never been farther from home than Washington, D.C., the vista had a story-book quality, indescribably foreign and exciting.

In the morning she had assured her mother that she'd be quite able to get off at the proper corner. "After all, I'm not a baby, Mother dear!" But now she wasn't quite so self-confident. The side streets skipped past at breath-taking speed, and every new block of buildings looked like all the rest. It was impossible to ask help from the driver, because Peggy knew no Portuguese, so finally she just picked a promising spot and trailed along behind some other descending passengers. Actually, as she discovered when she crossed the highway and could read the building numbers, she was about half a mile from home, but the walk seemed short, because there was so much to see.

In the apartment her mother was unpacking a trunk, which had been shipped on ahead, and murmuring a strange word over and over—*almoxarifado*—as though it might escape her if she stopped repeating it.

"*Almoxarifado* means storeroom in Brazilian," she told Peggy. "It's where this trunk came from and where it has to go back to." Then she dropped cross-legged to the floor, cradling a pile of linens in her lap, and looked up expectantly.

"It's a big school," Peggy said at once. "Much bigger than I thought it would be, and very new and modern looking." She parked her books on a nearby table and sat down on the floor opposite her mother. "There are kids from all over the world!"

"Did you meet anybody interesting?"

"Oh yes! I had lunch with a whole crowd." Peggy managed to describe Becky and Ann Tjian quite graphically, but when she came to Cleonice Andrade she found it more difficult. "The Brazilian girls seem older—and curvier. I guess you'd call them more mature."

Mrs. Jamison smiled. "You'll get curvy soon enough," she promised, looking with motherly affection at Peggy's slender, rather boyish figure. "But I know what you mean about Brazilian girls. They're more—well, I'd say more voluptuous."

Peggy nodded, although the word was one she never would have chosen. "Becky says they spend simply quantities of time getting their hair done and deciding what to wear. And there's another thing. She says they dress to please men!"

"Well, don't try to copy them," Mrs. Jamison advised. "Just be yourself—natural and fresh and friendly —and you'll get along."

Half-embarrassed, half-pleased at the compliment, Peggy wrinkled her nose and launched on a new subject. "Classes are really tough. They're way ahead in French—I mean of Country Day. And Portuguese! I'll never learn it—never! I'm absolutely sure."

"That makes two of us," her mother said companionably. Then she touched her forehead with the palm of her hand. "Good heavens, what was that word?"

"*Almoxarifado*," said Peggy with surprising speed, and they both laughed.

It occurred to Peggy, in an instant of insight, that her mother was going to have a few hurdles to cross, too. It wouldn't be easy to do the marketing, hire domestic help, or get the household running smoothly in a strange country. Yet the apartment was beginning to acquire a homelike air. The furniture had been shifted around; a few small ornaments, brought along in the trunk, had been strategically placed; and there were fresh flowers on one of the tables. Like all of the women in her family, Virginia Cullen had a talent for gracious living. She loved soft, pale colors and had decorated her home in Charlotte in yellows and greens. Here the white curtains were a challenge, but Peggy could already imagine the room burgeoning into a place which would eventually acquire her special signature.

As a matter of fact, her mother seemed to find the

change of scene refreshing. Although her brown hair was tumbled and her lipstick had worn off, she looked younger and prettier than usual.

"Have you been swimming?" Peggy asked.

Mrs. Jamison nodded. "This morning. Aren't you jealous? The water was marvelous—just cool enough!"

"Where's Tobey?"

"Still playing on the beach. Didn't you see him?" Mrs. Jamison got to her feet, balancing the linens gracefully, and dumped them in a chair on her way to the long windows that opened on a balcony facing the sea.

Peggy followed, and together the two searched the sand until they spotted a familiar skinny figure in striped shorts. "There he is," said Mrs. Jamison in mild relief. "He's been building a sand castle most of the afternoon."

"When does his school start?" asked Peggy a trifle enviously.

"Next Monday. We went to see about it today." Mrs. Jamison pushed back a lock of short hair, which had fallen to her forehead. "I wish I was as certain as your father that we're doing the right thing."

"You mean in putting him into a Brazilian school?"

Mrs. Jamison nodded. "Daddy is sure he'll learn the language twice as fast as the rest of us in this sink-or-swim way. But if anybody said to me, 'Learn Portuguese or sink,' I'm sure I'd go down like a stone."

"You're not eight years old," Peggy reminded her unnecessarily.

Her mother laughed. "You're so right."

Peggy turned away from the window. "Are we going to eat in or out?" she asked.

"Out," replied her mother promptly. "I decided not to try to cope with everything at once." She glanced down at her linen shorts and sleeveless shirt. "I'd better go bathe and change." As an afterthought she mentioned, "By the way, darling, you mustn't wear shorts, except right here at Copacabana."

Peggy looked up in surprise. "Why not?"

"I don't know. It isn't done, that's all," her mother replied vaguely. "When in Rome—"

The unfinished sentence hovered on the air inconsequentially, and as Mrs. Jamison left the room Peggy flung herself into an easy chair, her neck on one of its arms, her legs over the other. It had been a full day and she was suddenly tired, but not unhappy. Becky had been nice to squire her around and see that she got launched, and tomorrow was bound to be easier. She hoped she'd run into the boy they called Dom Carlos again, although the chances were slim, because he wasn't in any of her classes. She wondered if he was a junior or a senior, and suspected the latter, because he looked older. A faint smile touched her lips as she thought of Cleo's proprietary attitude and wondered if it was justified.

"Coming, darling? I'll start you a bath if you like. It takes forever! No wonder they complain about the water shortage in Rio. Is Tobey home yet?"

Peggy pulled herself together, went back to the

window, and looked out. "He's coming across the road now," she called. Then, as she went along the hall toward her bedroom, she asked, "Do you suppose Brazilian boys ever take American girls out on dates?"

She didn't wait for an answer to the question, because at that moment the telephone rang and she hurried back to answer it. "Daddy wants us to come see his office first, then go over to the American Club for dinner," she announced a few seconds later. "He says we should get a cab."

This wasn't an easy thing to do at six o'clock on the Avenida Atlântica, so the Jamisons walked inland a block, hoping for better luck. Everywhere the shops were still brightly lighted and the sidewalks were crowded with people—young and old, rich and poor, dark-skinned and fair. Street vendors hawked flowers, fountain pens, and junk jewelry along the curbs, while behind plate-glass windows gleamed Brazilian gems —aquamarines, amethysts, emeralds, tourmalines, to- pazes—set in platinum or gold.

Catching a glimpse of her own reflection as she stopped to admire a glittering display of stones, Peggy felt a sort of pleased surprise. In this foreign country she looked different to herself, more attractive, because her hair was so unusual among the brunet Cariocas, as the people who lived in Rio were called. She remembered an overheard remark made long ago by one of her mother's friends—"Peggy is going to be a very pretty girl"—and wondered fleetingly if it was true. There were so many girls who could never look forward to being even momentarily beautiful. They had the wrong kind of noses, or too many freckles, or receding chins. It would be nice, she thought, very nice—

"Margaret! Hurry, dear."

"Why does Daddy want us to see his office?" Peggy asked, as they climbed into the cab her mother had finally persuaded to stop.

"Because it's his, of course," Mrs. Jamison replied promptly. "And you must be admiring. The male ego is very tender, and should be treated accordingly."

But it was hard to be especially enthusiastic about a glass-walled series of offices on the nineteenth floor of a building that looked just like the one across the street. The furniture was contemporary, the floors were polished, the potted plants—used for accent, Mrs. Jamison said—were green and glossy. A couple of Mr. Jamison's assistants were still at their desks, and these men he introduced to his wife and children.

Peggy shook hands in turn with a Mr. Costa and a Mr. Pereira, the former owlish and skinny, with a sallow complexion, and the latter so dark that his skin seemed almost purple. She could see Tobey staring at him curiously, and knew exactly what he was thinking —that he could have come from the same family as their maid Delia back home.

Mrs. Jamison greeted each of the men courteously, but she didn't shake hands, as was the Brazilian custom. Alabama-bred, she didn't consider it correct for a lady to offer her hand to a strange gentleman, and

Peggy could tell that she was surprised that a Negro should be employed in a business office and accepted on the same terms as anyone else.

She mentioned this to her husband as they rode down in the self-service elevator, in which they were the only passengers. Charles Jamison just laughed, with a tolerance conditioned by his early years in New York public schools. "Brazil has little or no color line, remember."

"I'm starving," interrupted Tobey. "When do we eat?"

"Now," his father promised. "Right now. But instead of going to the Club, I'm going to take you to a real Brazilian restaurant on the roof of that department store right across the square."

"Oh, boy," said Tobey. "Let's go."

Soon another elevator let the family out on a lobby, backed by a trio of small *boutiques*, one selling hand-embroidered purses, another jewelry, and a third flowers. Chandeliers sparkled above and were repeated over the buffet in a long dining room, across which a headwaiter led the Jamisons to a table beside a glass wall, which looked over a panorama of winking lights. From the boulevard, stretching along the curved coast line to the mountains beyond the crowded buildings, the city glittered, and far off to the right, hanging as though suspended in the night sky, was the illuminated statue of Christ on top of the peak called the Corcovado, or Hunchback.

"It isn't surprising, is it, that Rio is called the *Cidade*

Maravilhosa?" asked Mr. Jamison of his wife and daughter, who were lost in admiration of the view, while Tobey studied the menu, frowning at the sudden realization that it was printed in Portuguese.

"The Marvelous City," Mrs. Jamison translated softly. "It would make a good title for a book."

A waiter, who could speak English, had appeared at the table, and for a few minutes, while her parents were occupied with ordering, Peggy sat and surveyed the room. The sort of well-to-do Brazilians who patronized a restaurant like this, she noticed, were dressed rather formally, the women frequently in black, with high-heeled pumps and hair coifed in the height of fashion, the men in dark suits and starched white shirts. In contrast, her mother was wearing a slim sheath of hyacinth-blue linen, and her father had on a striped shirt with his summer-weight gabardine.

A family group, dining a few tables away, particularly caught Peggy's attention. There was a girl facing her who looked distinctly familiar. Of course! She had sat next to her in French class and had admired her accent, although she couldn't recall having heard her name.

She would have pointed the girl out to her mother, but her parents had gone back to their discussion of Brazil and, unlike her younger brother, Peggy was too well-trained to interrupt.

"Originally," her father was saying, "there were three stocks—the Portuguese, who colonized the country and who already had a good deal of dark Moorish blood in their veins; the Africans, imported as slaves to work the sugar plantations; and the Indians, who had been here a good long time before."

Listening with only one ear, because her father was sounding too pedantic to be interesting, Peggy continued to regard the Brazilian family, who seemed to be enjoying not only their food but each other. The mother and father, sitting opposite one another, Peggy could see only in profile, but they looked relaxed and pleasant, and their son—she supposed it was their son whose back was toward her—was leaning forward and talking with animation to all three. Then the lad turned slightly, and Peggy's eyes widened in surprise as she recognized her cafeteria cavalier. Instinctively she sat a little straighter and touched her hair to be sure that it was smooth.

But all through dinner Carlos never once turned her way, and somehow it became pointless to explain to her parents that earlier in the day she had been handed a tray by a fellow student, now sitting across the room. Although Peggy slid an occasional glance in the direction of the other table, she returned a decent part of her attention to her own family group.

Then, as the Brazilians pushed back their chairs and rose to leave, Carlos looked around and, for a flicker of an instant, caught Peggy's eye. He didn't attempt to speak, and Peggy lowered her lashes to screen any sign of too-quick recognition, addressing herself to the last bit of food on her plate. Yet she was aware of the moment when he passed their table, and she dared to glance after him as he went through the dining-room door. His parents and the girl, who apparently was his younger sister, had stopped to talk with an elderly couple who were just arriving, but Carlos went on out into the lobby and disappeared from view.

Peggy put down her fork and relaxed her guard. Now she wished she had told her family that these Brazilian young people were schoolmates. Then it occurred to her suddenly that it was a trifle strange that Cariocas should be sent to the American School, and was curious concerning the reasons.

A bus boy was clearing the table now, and Tobey was consulting his father on a choice of desserts, when a waiter, carrying a single white orchid on a silver tray, suddenly appeared at Peggy's elbow.

"*Para a senhorita*," he said, with a slight bow.

Peggy flushed in surprised embarrassment. "Oh no," she said, shaking her head. "It must be for someone else."

But the waiter, baffled by the incomprehensible foreign language, was not to be put off. Since Peggy apparently did not intend to take the flower from the tray, he put the server down before her, bowed again, and went away.

All of the Jamisons stared at the orchid for a second or two as though it might suddenly rise and bite them. Then Mrs. Jamison, recovering her social poise as she became aware that diners at nearby tables were also interested, said to Peggy with a smile, "You'd better pin it on your frock, dear. It's very beautiful."

"But it isn't mine!" Peggy protested in a whisper.

"The waiter seemed very sure of himself," commented her father.

Tobey looked doubtful. "Who'd send *Peggy* a thing like that?" he inquired, with unflattering emphasis.

Peggy's cheeks flamed a deeper red, but not because of Tobey's gibe. It must have been Carlos, she was thinking. It's the only explanation. But what a very strange—what a *foreign*—thing to do.

She picked up the dewy-fresh flower, which was smaller than the cattleya orchids common in the United States, and pinned it high on the shoulder of her simple, round-necked green dress, where it looked like a small white bird ready to take flight.

"How fascinating to have a secret admirer!" her mother was murmuring in delight and amusement. "I'm purely envious. Ah, to be sixteen again."

Charles Jamison reached across the table and covered his wife's hand. "I'll buy you an orchid, *senhora,* any time you say."

"But don't you see—the fun is in *not* saying!" said Virginia.

Normally Peggy would have been amused by her parents' teasing, but tonight she gave the conversation only token attention. Far from being able to accept the gift casually, she was both mystified and excited by the incident. Maybe I'm wrong, she tried to tell herself. Maybe it was the manager of the restaurant or somebody, and not Carlos at all. She bent her head slightly to the side until the orchid petals brushed her cheek. They felt like starched velvet and made her think of a party dress she had owned when she was a little girl.

The flower looked lovely, she knew, against her green frock, and because it was her first orchid, she knew she would never forget it, no matter who had sent it.

But she did hope it was not the manager, or even worse, some silly old man who just happened to admire girls with red hair.

She wanted it to be Carlos! And if it was Carlos, Peggy thought in sudden alarm, how do I act when I see him again?

Chapter 3

As it happened, Peggy did not see Carlos all the next day, but because the teacher—a Mademoiselle Chaligny—was late for French class, she made the acquaintance of his sister.

The girls weren't actually introduced, but since they sat next to one another it was natural that they should talk while they were waiting, and after a few minutes Peggy's neighbor said, "I'm Margarida Almeida, although everyone calls me Guida. You're Margaret Jamison, aren't you? I remember your name from the list of new students, because it's so much like mine."

Peggy nodded and smiled, although she felt wary. If Carlos had sent the orchid, did Guida know? As she turned her clever, thin, fine-drawn face toward Peggy, certainly nothing in the expression presented a clue.

"You were at Mesbla last night, weren't you?" continued Guida.

"Yes," Peggy said shyly. "I saw you, too."

"We were going to a concert," Guida vouchsafed, speaking such fluent English that Peggy was scarcely aware she was foreign. "My father thinks music is very important and he always takes us along."

"Don't you like music?" asked Peggy.

Guida shrugged, her black eyes suddenly mischievous. "I'm almost tone deaf to classical music," she admitted, "but I do like the popular records we get from the States."

"I brought a few with me," Peggy said, with increasing interest. "Some musical comedies, a new Belafonte, and an old Paul Anka recording or two. Maybe you'd like to come up to the apartment some afternoon," she added impulsively, "and let me play them for you."

"I'd love to," Guida said, "if you don't live too far away. Mother is fussy about the time I get home." She pursed her lips and skillfully imitated the adult point of view. "Young girls of good family should never be seen on the street after dusk."

Peggy chuckled. "Our mothers sound a little alike," she told Guida. "We come from the South—"

At that moment the teacher arrived, looking harried and indignant that her pupils should be chattering so unrestrainedly. "*Bon jour, mes enfants,*" she said, then more loudly, "*bon jour, classe!*"

"*Bon jour, Mademoiselle,*" echoed the class, including Guida and Peggy, who twisted around and straightened themselves in their seats.

I like Guida, thought Peggy. I like her enormously! And she knew that this feeling had nothing to do with Carlos. Guida was endearing, provocative, spontaneously gay. She was different enough to be intriguing, yet Peggy knew already that they shared a similar sense of humor, and that they would be friends.

She lunched with Becky and her crowd again, but she looked on them with a more critical eye. Of the group, Becky was the most forthright and likeable. Linda Paul seemed increasingly nondescript. Ann Tjian, the Chinese girl, was so quiet and different that it was impossible to judge what she might be like on further acquaintance, but she felt that the Portuguese girl could be assessed fairly accurately. Cleo was the sort who resented any competition, and who mistrusted any female who was half as attractive as she.

She watched Peggy covertly throughout the meal, then pushed back her plate, leaned forward on her elbows, and said, "Your hair's a wonderful color—really it is! But doesn't it take a lot of doing?"

Peggy shook her head. "I set it myself."

Cleo tilted an eyebrow and gave a throaty laugh. "I was talking about the *color*."

Genuinely astonished, Peggy said, "I don't dye my hair."

"Oh, come now," Cleo teased. "There's nothing to be ashamed of."

"But I don't." Belatedly, Peggy realized that she was being baited, and forced herself to grin with an appearance of good nature. "Though I may be forced to," she added, "if people in Rio are so suspicious of redheads. What color would be becoming?" She turned to the other girls. "Dark brown?"

"*Touché*," murmured Becky, with a chuckle, and Peggy grinned at her appreciatively. Cleo settled back in her chair without pursuing the question, and Ann Tjian glanced from one to the other, baffled but expressionless.

After lunch the girls wandered off on various errands, Ann and Linda to the library, Cleo to the courtyard where the boys usually congregated, Becky to the office in search of a lost book.

"Let's get together over the week end," Becky suggested cordially to Peggy before she left the table. "Usually there's a crowd from school on the beach."

Would the crowd from school include Carlos? Peggy's heart leaped at the thought, and at once she wondered whether the white orchid, now reposing in the apartment refrigerator, was still fresh.

"We usually meet in front of the Copa Palace about ten-thirty," Becky was saying. "How does that sound to you?"

"Fine, just fine!" Peggy agreed at once, feeling fortunate to be included.

But when she arrived at the appointed spot on Saturday morning she was rather disappointed to find only Linda Paul and Becky awaiting her. They were stretched out on straw mats in the shade of an umbrella, but Peggy put her beach towel down in the sun.

"Take it easy," Becky cautioned. "Even brunettes turn watermelon pink if they're not careful."

Peggy started to rub her skin with sun-tan oil. "What do you recommend? Half an hour the first day?"

Linda looked up. "You're lucky not to have the kind of skin that usually goes with red hair. Me—I burn just terribly. I have to keep wrapped up like a cocoon."

The long combers, rolling in to the beach, were beautiful and inviting, and this sort of conversation made Peggy yawn. After a few minutes she stood up and stretched, and then, since Becky had her eyes closed, wandered down alone to the water's edge.

The ocean was just cool enough to be inviting, and she decided to go for a swim, although she had left her bathing cap in her beach bag. Wading into the surf, she dove straight through the first high comber and came up on the other side, heading with an easy crawl toward deeper water.

She turned on her back and floated for a few minutes, utterly relaxed, intensely glad to be exactly where she was. Rio was bound to be a great experience, especially with a boy like Carlos hovering in the background. Given luck and a modicum of patience, she could have a marvelous year.

The modicum of patience was necessary more quickly than Peggy had bargained for. Having ridden a few waves and waded ashore once more, she was wringing out her soaked hair when she realized that the group under and around the beach umbrella had swelled. Two Texas boys from her biology class—Fred Perkins and Chuck Whiteside—had joined the girls. They were sprawled characteristically on the sand, while standing talking to them was a trio instantly recognizable as Guida, Carlos, and Cleo.

Peggy wished she had been less transported by the lure of the ocean. Cleo, in a barebacked white *maillot*, looked absolutely ravishing, while she herself looked like a wet cocker spaniel. She considered retreating into the waves once more, but it was too late. Guida had spotted her and was beckoning, then running toward her. "*Bom dia*, Peggy. I want you to meet my brother." A moment later she was saying, "Carlinhos, this is Margaret Jamison, the girl I was telling you about."

Soaking wet, her hair plastered to her head and her eyes slightly bloodshot from peering through salt water, Peggy felt anything but attractive. She stood her ground, however, while Carlos turned and swept her with a glance that betrayed a certain amusement. "And this is Cleonice Andrade, *senhorita*."

Stunned by such formality in a teen-ager, Peggy murmured her nickname automatically and then said, "Cleo and I already know one another. We met at school."

"We've even lunched together," drawled Cleo, as she adjusted the strap of her bathing suit, then wearily added, "twice."

It was like a slap in the face. In spite of herself, Peggy flinched. Then, to cover her chagrin, she burst out laughing. "You make it sound like a penance, Cleo, honestly!"

There was no recourse for the other girl but an apology. "*Desculpe*," she murmured in Portuguese, although she didn't look sorry. She looked as though she was anxious to move on.

However, the two Almeidas lingered, making casual conversation. "It's a perfect day for a surfboard," Guida commented, shading her eyes with one hand as she examined the waves. "We've got one with us, Margaret—Peggy, I mean—if you want to borrow it."

Interest and uncertainty flickered in Peggy's expression. "I've never used one," she admitted, "but I'd love to try."

"Do you water ski?" asked Carlos.

"Yes."

"You won't have any trouble. I'll take you out and show you."

"That would be awfully nice!" Peggy said quickly, without glancing at Cleo to see how she was reacting to this proposal. Would Carlos take this opportunity, she wondered, to explain the mystery of the orchid? The question was so tantalizing that she felt she couldn't bear to have it go unanswered. Yet, now that she was face to face with this boy, she felt sure she could never bring it up herself.

"We've got our things just up the beach," said Guida. Then she suggested, "Why don't we move them down here?"

By the time the trio returned, the group had grown even larger. Another Brazilian boy, carrying a beach ball, had joined the crowd, and his two younger sisters, wearing brief bikinis and with small gold buttons in their pierced ears, had stopped to invite the Texas boys to go for a walk.

Peggy tried to conceal the fact that she was shocked. No North Carolina girl would dream of appearing in public in such scanty attire, nor would one have been so conspicuously flirtatious. She knew exactly what her mother would call these sisters—"forward"—yet the rest of the group seemed to accept their behavior as perfectly natural. Inevitably, Peggy felt confused.

It crossed her mind that she had heard Brazil called a country of contrasts, and she decided that this must be true on several counts. It was considered improper to wear shorts, yet bikinis were not uncommon. Manners could be so formal they were positively quaint, or the lack of them could seem actually brazen. It made Peggy feel uncertain, as though she were treading on eggs.

She was relieved to break loose and follow Carlos and Guida into the ocean. Cleo, who had borrowed the beach ball and was playfully tossing it into the air, refused Carlos' invitation to join them. "I think I'll wait until later," she said, with no conspicuous rancor. Apparently she had decided it was better to accept the situation and bide her time.

Carlos pushed the surfboard through the first breaking waves, then propelled it to deeper water by lying aboard and doing a flutter kick. To Peggy, swimming after him, he looked as brown, as lean, and as muscular as a beach boy in an Hawaiian travel ad. Jim Barton paled to insignificance by comparison.

Carlos turned the board, grinned at the two girls, and said, "The trick is to catch a wave just right." He glanced behind, readied himself, and a second later was skimming in to the beach on the crest of a fast-moving comber. The maneuver looked so graceful and so effortless that Peggy was filled with anticipation. "I can hardly wait to try it!" she called to Guida. "But it can't be as easy as it looks."

This presentiment proved correct. In spite of Carlos' coaching, Peggy caught the first wave wrong, felt the board being wrenched out of her grip, and went hurtling along in its wake of roiling water. Next time she was more careful and managed to get a short but satisfactory ride, and on the third try she soared in to the beach as Carlos had, high and fast on a long roller.

"You take it now. It's your turn," Peggy called to Guida as she brought the board back. She pushed the wet hair from her forehead and smiled in delight at Carlos. "Thanks a lot. It's great fun, isn't it?"

The Brazilian boy nodded, pleased. "You picked it up quickly." Then he added, "I was sure you would."

"Why were you sure?" asked Peggy, treading water. She was honestly curious.

"Because it's easy to see you're just naturally athletic. The way you walk, the way you swim, the way you aren't afraid to try something new."

"Well, thank you!" Peggy knew this was a compliment to treasure, because it meant that Carlos had been more aware of her than she might have guessed.

She saw a comber building up to a perfect size and caught it as it broke, riding it in, then scrambled to her feet in the shallow water. Carlos, right beside her, shook the water out of his eyes, then said, "Don't run away."

"I'm not," Peggy protested, but she had been, almost instinctively. The boy should be the pursuer, the girl the pursued.

Carlos was laughing. "You're very refreshing," he murmured. "Why haven't you thanked me for the orchid, by the way?"

"You *did* send it!" Peggy cried spontaneously. "Oh, I do thank you! It was beautiful, and it lasted three whole days."

Carlos grinned. "I'm glad you liked it. It was fun wondering what you were thinking, and if you'd guessed."

This admission, both surprising and intriguing, Peggy cherished for the rest of the morning. It made up for the perfection of Cleo's appearance, for her own lank hair, and for the fact that Carlos paid her no special attention once they had rejoined the crowd. She took Becky's advice and stayed safely in the shade of the umbrella until it was time to go home for lunch, then said her good-by's swiftly, hoping that she had made a sufficiently good impression to be included again.

Guida came running after her as she started along the beach. "I'll walk part way with you," she said companionably, and fell into step by Peggy's side.

For a few minutes the girls made desultory conversation. "Do you think you'll like Rio?" Guida asked. Then, without waiting for an answer, she added, "Does it seem very different from the United States?"

Peggy nodded, laughing. "Very."

"How?" Guida probed.

This was a difficult question to answer, if a person had never seen the other country. Peggy fumbled for a few seconds, then hit on the idea of trying to explain the situation of bikinis versus shorts.

Guida didn't understand at all. "*I* don't wear a bikini," she objected. "And the Copacabana girls who do are considered a bit forward. Still, they are on the beach, and they are going swimming. While on the street—well, my mother thinks slacks are bad enough, but she says no woman looks attractive in short pants!"

Peggy thought of her own mother, who looked like a Southern gentlewoman no matter what she had on, but she didn't pursue the subject, because at that moment her attention was caught by a crowd forming along the tide line farther down the beach. Three fishing boats were lying offshore, well beyond the breakers, while a number of men seemed to be pulling something up onto the beach. "What's happening?" she asked.

"They're drag seining," Guida replied promptly, then urged, "let's hurry," and broke into a run. "It's interesting to watch."

Joining the group of spectators, Peggy could see that the men had drawn a huge net in a circle around a

school of fish, and were now engaged in hauling it in
to dry land. In the shallow surf she could see the silver
bodies of fish jumping and thrashing, fighting to free
their entangled gills, while the lean, bronzed fisher-
men brought the sides of the net inexorably closer.

Some of the men wore straw hats, but most were
naked from the waist up, and their muscles looked
hard as steel. Squinting in the strong sun, and working
without concern for the growing crowd, they looked as
though they belonged to a different breed from the
beach loungers. Some were very black, with Negroid
features, and others had the brown skin and straight
hair that spoke of Indian blood. A few had the slight,
wiry bodies of Portuguese, and one had slanted, Ori-
ental eyes. Peggy was reminded of her father's description of the blending of races and thought it
couldn't be better illustrated, but Guida was concerned
only with the fish.

"Not much of a catch," was her opinion, as the net
was dragged above the tide line. "You'll see much
better shows than this." She turned aside, then stopped
to speak to a couple who stood, arms across one another's shoulders, by the water's edge. She greeted
them in Portuguese, *"Bom dia!"* murmured a few words
Peggy didn't understand, then turned with a quick
"Desculpe," and introduced her new friend.

"This is Margaret Jamison," she said in English.
"Josefina and Roberto Santos. They are neighbors of
ours."

Peggy scarcely caught the names, because she was

too struck by their appearance. The girl, who might have been eighteen, had long black hair, pinned up in a French twist, eyes like black velvet, and coffee-colored skin, while her companion was as fair as Peggy herself. They were both extremely gracious, shaking hands and murmuring polite phrases in school-book English, while Guida stood by happily, as though she had produced Peggy for their special benefit.

She said, as they left to go on their way, "Aren't they sweet together? They've just been married, and they're very much in love."

"Married?" Peggy's surprise colored her voice. "They seem awfully young," she said, glancing after them, then added, "hasn't she the most gorgeous tan!"

"Tan?" Guida swung around to look back. "Josefina's not especially tan. But her skin *is* a beautiful color, isn't it? I'd never noticed before how washed-out Roberto looks by comparison."

Peggy was still pondering this remark as she rode up in the apartment elevator, having left Guida to walk back up the beach alone. She could imagine the shocked and censorious stares such a couple would receive on the streets of Charlotte. The very fact that Josefina was striking, with the long, graceful legs and slender neck of a fashion model, would make her doubly conspicuous and open to criticism. Mother, thought Peggy, would consider her a mulatto. She smiled to herself, glad at least that she had been raised in a North Carolina city rather than a small Alabama town. There were some things about Brazil, she realized, that would be a little difficult to accept.

In the apartment, things were in a state of happy confusion. Tobey was lying sprawled on the sofa reading a comic magazine brought all the way from Idlewild Airport, Mr. Jamison was prying open a carton of books, and Mrs. Jamison was making sandwiches in the kitchen.

"Guess what!" she called, the moment Peggy opened the door. "We've got a maid—and by the most marvelous stroke of luck, a maid who can speak English. A godsend, I must say! She's been working for a Baptist missionary family, who brought her to Rio when they moved from Salvador, and now the missionary has been transferred to Africa or somewhere and Jacinta is coming to work for us."

Charles Jamison sat back on his heels and laughed. "Your mother is now able to take a new lease on life. Notice how much less careworn she looks?"

"It isn't funny, Charles. It's purely providential. Besides, I told you Mother raised her girls to be helpless, so they'd marry rich men."

Mr. Jamison, snorting derisively, went back to unpacking his books, but Peggy said, "That's lovely, Mother. When does she start?"

"Monday." Mrs. Jamison glanced around the disheveled kitchen, which she did not consider her province. "I can hardly wait!"

Jacinta proved to be every bit as much of a godsend as Mrs. Jamison had anticipated. She was a tall, statuesque woman who followed the custom of old-fashioned servants from the state of Bahia and wound her head with a turban. Instead of a uniform she wore a full skirt of printed cotton and short-sleeved, round-necked blouses. Her aprons were starched and immaculate, and to Peggy and Tobey she looked like an oversized Aunt Jemima doll.

In short order she took over the running of the Jamison household. Early in the morning she did the marketing, then made the beds and dusted the rooms, moving slowly and majestically through the apartment with mop and sweeper. But it was her kitchen that was Jacinta's true castle. She was enchanted by its efficiency, compared to the antiquated cookroom in which she had previously worked, and from midafternoon on, the fragrance of her baking drifted through the door. To the Jamisons' delight, she prepared many of her native Bahian dishes, spicy and aromatic. They were introduced to *vatapá*, a casserole made of tiny shrimps and coconut milk, thickened with manioc meal and made biting with peppers, and to a thick and viscid okra soup, which tasted something like a New Orleans gumbo.

By the time another week end rolled around, the family was really beginning to "settle in," as Mrs. Jamison put it. Tobey had philosophically accepted his school and the problem of conquering a strange language, although he objected to the teachers' calling

him by his full name, Matthew. He adapted himself to
Rio even faster than Peggy, and astonished his parents
by conducting beach conversations with his contem-
poraries in a kind of pidgin Portuguese.

On Friday afternoon Peggy brought Guida home
with her, as she had promised, and the two girls listened to records and were plied with Jacinta's home-
made cakes, which she called *doces*, brought in on a
tray along with glasses of fresh pineapple juice. Mrs.
Jamison, who had been lunching with an acquaintance
from the Embassy staff, arrived home with her arms
full of fresh flowers just as Guida was leaving, so the
two had a chance to meet.

Peggy, introducing her new acquaintance to her
mother, felt a glow of pride. In a gray linen suit and
high-heeled black pumps, with her fluffy hair a tou-
sled halo around her animated face, Mrs. Jamison
looked both youthful and chic. She greeted Guida
warmly, and commented, the moment the Brazilian
girl had left, "She's delightful—a pixie, really. How
nice that you should be finding friends."

"I'm glad you liked her," Peggy said, as she helped
arrange the flowers in two fat white bowls. Then she
added confidentially, "She has an older brother who's
one of the best-looking boys I've ever seen."

"Aha!" commented Mrs. Jamison. "When do I get
to meet him?"

Peggy grinned but flushed in spite of herself. "I've
found out that in Rio boys don't date the way they do

at home," she replied a trifle disconsolately. "I mean they don't go out *alone* to the movies or anything. But tomorrow Guida says her crowd may be having a beach picnic. And she's going to telephone and invite me. At least, so she says."

Chapter 4

Since, thus far, the telephone in the apartment had rung only when her father was calling from the office, Peggy was quite unprepared for the maddening inefficiency of a communication system she had always accepted as foolproof.

At the very first squeak of the bell, early on Saturday morning, she raced for the receiver and was rewarded for a fraction of a second by a distant, indistinct, but unmistakable voice. "Hello, Peggy?"

"Guida!" Peggy felt a tremor of happy anticipation. "Hello."

But by now the line was dead. Having said a series of hello's, which rose in pitch with her growing indignation, Peggy hung up and sat beside the telephone, sure that she would be called right back. But five minutes passed, then ten, and when the bell finally rang again, her answer got no human response whatever, only a concentrated and infuriating buzzing.

Instead of going to the beach as she had planned, Peggy dawdled around the apartment all morning, waiting hopefully for Guida to call back. She even looked up the Almeida name in the Rio directory, but she wasn't sure either of Guida's father's name or of her exact address. Unfortunately, there were several Almeidas listed in Leblon, the section where the family lived.

By noon Peggy had almost given up hope, but at the eleventh hour the doorbell rang, and a messenger delivered an envelope, addressed to Senhorita Margaret Jamison. In it was an anxious note from Guida, explaining that she hadn't been able to "get through," but hoped Peggy could join a group planning to swim and cook a picnic supper at a small beach out near the Gavea Country Club.

"Wear your bathing suit under a blouse and skirt," Guida instructed, "and take one of the *lotações* (We call them *lotes* for short, but I think you call them buses) that go along the Avenida Atlântica to the Estrada da Barra." She gave full instructions on where to get off, and added, "Bring a sweater and towel but don't bother about food. We will have everything." Then, in a postscript, she scribbled, "If your mother is the sort who worries about chaperones the way mine does, tell her Josefina and Roberto will be along. They're married, remember, so that should be good enough."

Peggy dressed for the picnic with special care. She had washed her hair and set it on rollers early in the morning, and as she brushed it to shining perfection she promised herself to keep it dry and presentable no

matter if it meant missing a really good swim. To com-
pete with anyone as ravishing as Cleo Andrade was
going to be difficult enough, without the handicap of
looking like a drowned rat.

The bus ride was long and worrisome to Peggy, because she wasn't at all sure she could make the driver
understand where she wanted to get off. Becky had
told her a dismaying story of her early days in Rio,
when a bus she had thought was headed downtown
went straight up a mountain and stayed there for an
hour and forty-five minutes before coming down again.
But although the vehicle in which Peggy rode made
a habit of ducking back from the beach and racing
through an occasional tunnel, it always emerged
within sight of the ocean again. Eventually Peggy
caught sight of a likely group of young people standing in a huddle beside the road, and descended with
as much aplomb as though she had never had a moment's concern.

Guida and Carlos greeted her with relieved shouts,
and Becky grabbed her beach bag and insisted on
carrying it to a sandy cove, half-hidden by a rocky
promontory. Trailing along with them were several
North American boys and girls from school; a visiting
Argentine from Buenos Aires, whose name Peggy didn't
catch; two friends of Carlos', named Flávio and Luís;
and their younger sister, nicknamed Leninha.

Josefina and Roberto were coming a little later,
Guida mentioned, but she offered no explanation for
the fact that Cleo was nowhere in sight. Finally

Peggy's curiosity overcame her. "Is Cleo coming later too?"

Guida shook her head, saying, "She had a late appointment at the dentist today," while Peggy glanced at Carlos from under lowered lashes to see whether any flicker of disappointment crossed his face. But he seemed to be utterly unconcerned by Cleo's absence. His smile seemed to say that he would change nothing about the afternoon.

Some of the boys immediately began to gather driftwood on the deserted beach for the fire they would build later, but Carlos, who was carrying his surfboard, wanted no part of such dull work. "Come for a swim," he invited Peggy with unexpected urgency.

"Wait 'til I get my cap."

"No!" Carlos rapped out the word peremptorily. "Swim without one, the way you did last Saturday. I like to see your hair in the sun."

Peggy, who had been reaching for her beach bag, stopped as though frozen, like a living statue in the very act of motion. Never in her life had a boy spoken to her with such command. With a single remark, Carlos made her feel utterly feminine and desirable. With the very inflection of his voice, he had managed to tell her he was *glad* Cleo had stayed away.

Obedient, capless, her heart hammering against her ribs in a strange, thrilling excitement, Peggy followed Carlos into the sea. At the moment she would have followed him to the River Styx, had he invited her, so captivating did he seem.

For ten minutes or more the pair had the Atlantic to themselves, with the sun sparkling on the water and the group on the beach no more obtrusive than a cluster of cardboard characters in a toy theater. Peggy and Carlos rode the board a couple of times, then left it at the tide line, and swam back to deep water to float on the undulating swells.

They didn't talk much, but Peggy felt that at last she was really living. An island, shimmering in the distance, could have been Bali Ha'i, the mountain-rimmed coast a poet's dream, the sheltered beach a port of paradise. Rio de Janeiro, Rio de Janeiro, her heart sang—and she was only vaguely aware that she felt so lyrical because of Carlos.

He turned in the water, dove, and came up close beside Peggy, playful as a young porpoise. She laughed at him and he caught her hand. "Happy?" he asked.

"Very."

"So am I. I like you."

Daringly, Peggy confessed, "I like you, too."

The others were running into the water now, and by unspoken consent the two allowed themselves to drift down the beach until they could come in to shore at the very end, as alone as they could ever be in this little cove. They lay on the rocks, watching the swimmers idly, and Peggy shook her wet hair out in the sun.

Carlos reached over and touched it, remarking almost wistfully, "I wish Brazilian girls had hair like that."

Feeling bold beyond belief, Peggy replied, "I'm glad they haven't—if you like mine."

She turned on her stomach, pretending to be drowsy, but she kept stealing looks at the boy beside her, so bronzed and beautiful, like the statue of the young David in the museum at home. It seemed incredible to her now that she could have wasted a moment's regret on Jim Barton. Laurette King could have the lad, and welcome to him. She didn't care a fig if she never saw him again.

The only thing that mattered was Carlos, Carlos here and now; may tomorrow never come! If only she could lengthen this minute into an hour, the hour into a day, the day into a week, a month, a year.

"Sleepy?" Carlos asked.

"Mmm, not really."

"Good, because Guida's heading for us. She feels we should gather round and be social, I can tell."

Peggy didn't demur. She let Carlos help her to her feet and greeted his sister with a smile. "Coming, Mother!" she called teasingly. Then she cried, "Oh, it's so wonderful you two can speak English! I never imagined having such luck."

"Nevertheless, you're going to learn Portuguese," said Carlos sternly. "We ought to make a rule, Guida —from now on, English on Saturdays, Portuguese on Sundays."

"Does that mean I'm going to see you Sundays?" questioned Peggy, in mock innocence. "How nice!"

"You're frivolous," Carlos scolded. "Just like us Cari-ocas—a sybarite."

"What's a sybarite?" asked Peggy.

"Don't tell her, Guida! We know one English word she doesn't know."

"I know one Portuguese word you'd never guess," bragged Peggy. "*Almoxarifado*. I learned it almost the first day!"

Chattering inconsequentially, the trio arrived at the picnic place. Becky and some of the other girls were spreading out beach towels and blankets, Flávio and Luís were fanning a feeble thread of flame into a fire, while Josefina and Roberto, who had just arrived, were planning to go for a quick dip.

The sun, strong and warm ten minutes before, had ducked behind the cliff, and the thought of food was definitely inviting. "What can I do?" Peggy offered quickly, anxious to make amends for staying away so long.

Becky set her to work splitting and buttering a bag-ful of crusty Brazilian rolls. The picnic was to be an international affair—American hamburgers and Coke, Brazilian sausage and *guaraná*, with fruit and *doces* for dessert. Two of the other girls had washed the fruit in the ocean and were arranging it in a flat basket. To Peggy, watching as she worked, it looked colorful and tempting, but much of it was strange.

Guida and Becky supervised the cooking of the hamburgers and sausages. Then the picnickers helped themselves, and gathered in the usual happy confusion on the lee side of the fire. To Peggy it would have seemed much like a picnic at home, were it not for the medley of languages being spoken and the fact that after supper paper containers were produced and everyone sat around drinking cup after cup of *cafè-zinho,* a thick dark brew, half coffee, half sugar, which Peggy found distinctly unpalatable.

The boys were discussing Brazilian *futebol,* or soccer, amusingly pronounced "fuchyball," when Carlos tossed his empty coffee cup into the fire and came over to Peggy. "Let's take a walk," he suggested, "unless you're terribly interested."

Together they wandered down to the tide line and along the beach to the wet gray rocks where they had sunned only a couple of hours before. Again, amazingly, Peggy felt no compulsion to conduct a superficial conversation. She was comfortable with Carlos, in spite of the fact that she scarcely knew him. Instinctively, she realized that he felt the same way about her.

Then he startled her by asking, "How long are you going to be here?"

"Here? Where?"

"In Rio."

"A year," Peggy said. "Maybe more. Unless Daddy is transferred again."

"Back to the States?" For some reason Carlos looked hopeful.

But Peggy shook her head. "No. I think we'll be in

Brazil for two years at least." She hesitated, then asked, "Why?"

Carlos treated this as a rhetorical question requiring no answer. He picked up a pebble and skipped it over the water. "At night," he said, "the ocean's likely to be phosphorescent. When you swim you have a sparkly bright tail, like a comet. It's fun."

But Peggy changed the subject again. "Carlos, why do you and Guida go to the American School?"

"Because we're going to the United States to college."

"Guida too?" Already, Peggy knew that Brazilian girls seldom went away to college.

Carlos nodded. "My father has strong opinions on the subject. He says if you educate a man you educate an individual, but if you educate a woman you educate a whole family. And our Brazilian families are *big!*"

"Where will you go? To college, I mean." Peggy thought wishfully of Duke or the University of Virginia—anywhere in the South!

"I don't know," Carlos confessed, with a certain concern. "My father and one of my uncles went to Harvard, so they think that's the only place. But it depends." He skipped another stone and added, "I'll have a better idea after I take my college boards."

In any event, Peggy realized, Carlos would be going away next fall. Fall in the United States, but spring in Brazil—just about this time. She squatted on the edge of a rocky tide pool and pretended to be examining the shells clinging to the sides, while Carlos stood looking down at her contemplatively.

"You know," he said, after a moment or two, "a year has never seemed so short to me before. Never."

The innuendo was more in his tone of voice than in his actual words, but it was obvious that Peggy, although pleased, was embarrassed. To cover her confusion she pointed to a curious shell, attached to a submerged rock, and asked, "What's this? I've never seen one before."

Carlos knelt beside her and peered into the water. "You don't mean the limpets?"

"No, this."

"Oh, that's a chiton—a coat-of-mail shell," replied Carlos promptly. "See, it has eight overlapping pieces of armor—always the same number. You can count them."

Peggy complied without much enthusiasm. The shell had been introduced as a cover up, a subterfuge. Carlos, however, had suddenly become interested. "You know, it's curious," he said, "but scientists say these chitons are very primitive—that they're a lot like prehistoric animals, actually." He stopped short, as though caught in the act of being serious. "Am I boring you?"

"No," Peggy fibbed, rearranging her expression. It would never do to have Carlos consider her uninquisitive or dull. But she scarcely listened as he went on talking. The words he spoke became submerged in the consciousness of his physical presence, the manner he had of holding his head slightly sideways, the downy dark hairs on his forearm, the way his shirt stretched taut across his back.

"You aren't listening," he accused, then suddenly pulled her back from where she was balancing on her toes, to sit on the slippery rock, close against him for a moment. He laughed at her. "You weren't listening at all!"

Peggy moved away, pretending to be indignant. "I was too."

"What was I saying, then?"

But she couldn't tell him, and it suddenly struck them both as uproariously funny, and they leaned against one another and laughed some more. "You know," said Carlos, when he could catch his breath, "I think you have the most infectious laugh I've ever heard."

The twilight deepened into dusk, and smudgy silhouettes began to move around the dead fire in the distance. The picnickers were packing up.

"Time to go home," Carlos said, but he didn't move until Josefina started calling. "Has it *ever* been the right time to go home?" he asked grumpily. Then, with a characteristically quick change of mood, he smiled and said, "Anyway, I'm glad we're both going to be here for a while!"

Chapter 5

Peggy was glad too. In fact, she was deliriously grateful that it was to Rio de Janeiro that her father had been sent, and as a result she treated him with unusual pride and affection for several days. She also wrote exuberantly to Laurette and made an effort to describe Carlos Almeida, but found English adjectives inadequate.

"You'd have to *see* him to understand. Besides being perfectly knock-out looking, he's terribly *polite*," she burbled. "We had the most *divine* beach picnic last week end on this secluded, *empty* little beach, with a fire and everything. The only thing is, he's a senior, and he's going to the States to college—probably Harvard—next year. He's eighteen but he looks even older. Brazilian boys *do*.

"Tomorrow is Independence Day—the independence of Brazil, I mean. Like our Fourth of July, sort of. Daddy has a car now, and we're going to go up the mountain called the Corcovado (there's a road, I guess) and have lunch in a restaurant on the top.

Mother says I can invite Guida (that's Carlos' sister and she's terribly nice, we're *very* good friends already) and Carlos, too, if I want to. I'd adore it, of course, even if it *is* with the family, but I can't quite get up my nerve."

Peggy wrote this letter during a morning study period, in which she was presumably working at one of the partitioned desks in the fifth-floor library. Then she leaned on one hand and managed to strengthen her courage sufficiently to approach Guida as they again waited for Mademoiselle Chaligny, who was becoming habitually late for her French class.

"Are you doing anything special tomorrow?" she asked.

Guida shook her head. "Usually we have some sort of family party, but Mama is in bed with *la grippe*."

Peggy's heart skipped a beat, but she kept her voice carefully casual as she suggested, "We're going sightseeing, now that Daddy has a car. If it wouldn't bore you to death, why don't you and Carlos come along as guides? We'll have lunch at a restaurant someplace, and then Daddy will drive you home."

Guida looked thoughtful. "Have you said anything to Carlinhos?"

"No," Peggy confessed, feeling as though she were wearing her heart on her sleeve, when she should have been at pains to tuck it under her French book. "Even if Carlos can't come, of course I'd like you to come anyway."

"I'll try. I'll speak to Mama and phone you tonight,"

Guida promised, as Mademoiselle hurried breathlessly into the room. Chary of the unpredictable telephone system, Peggy's face fell, but she had to stifle her disappointment and hope for the best.

The best was positively superlative. Guida's voice was clear as a bell when she announced over the wire that both she and Carlos would be delighted to accept. If there was a faint note of surprise in the way she lingered over her brother's name, Peggy chose to ignore it. "That's marvelous," she said, and made the necessary arrangements, glad that Guida proposed that she and Carlos could walk over to the apartment more readily than she could give directions to the Almeida house.

Now a new sort of nervousness attacked Peggy. She was flooded with concern that her family would make a poor showing in front of the Brazilian boy. At breakfast the next morning she objected to her father's tweed jacket, because it was too sporty; she insisted that Tobey should wear a white shirt and tie, instead of the round-necked jersey which he considered holiday attire; and she even criticized the fact that her mother was wearing flat heels.

The male members of the family snorted and fumed at such caviling, but Mrs. Jamison was unexpectedly understanding. She looked at her husband and son and said, "Just this once, why don't we humor Peggy? Brazilians do dress differently, and we don't want to seem out of step."

But even with the clothes problem corrected, Peggy

continued to worry. As the hour for the Almeidas' arrival approached she was filled with regret that she had ever invited them at all. Her father's crew cut, she decided, made him look ridiculous—like a super-annuated collegian—and her mother's hair flew every which way, because she never used the lacquer with which Brazilian women kept their coiffures impeccable. As for Tobey—well, Tobey was frankly impossible. He had bitten his fingernails to the quick, he couldn't keep his face clean for ten minutes, and he kept talking constantly, about nothing. It was almost too much to bear!

Peggy's anxiety might have precipitated a family feud had not Jacinta stepped into the breach. "*Senhorita*—little pigeon!" she called softly from the kitchen. "Come and talk a moment with me."

Her face clouded with distress, Peggy stamped out of the living room, but the mere presence of the *baiana*, statuesque and dignified as she turned from the sink, exerted a calming influence.

In a tone of comfort rather than reprimand, Jacinta said, "I don't know these friends of yours, but I've worked for a highborn Brazilian family in my time, and they had North Americans come to their house some. Do you know what it was about these folks from the States the Brazilians liked? They liked them because they were so natural, and they liked them because they were different. It may well be, child, that your friends will like the *senhor* and the *senhora*—and yes, even our little Tobey—just as they are."

At the moment Peggy was too edgy to admit that Jacinta's words gave her pause, but she went into the bathroom, recombed her hair, and stopped gritting her teeth. When she came out to answer the door she wore a manufactured but superficially sunny smile.

Fortunately, it took almost no time at all for Jacinta's prediction to prove correct. The young Almeidas, with their good manners and gaiety, quite captivated Mr. and Mrs. Jamison, and in turn the enthusiasm of the North American family concerning the beauties of their native city made the Cariocas feel proud and happy. It was a very successful outing indeed.

Even Tobey reacted to the presence of these new acquaintances and stopped chattering inconsequentially, interrupting only to ask a really important question or two. He consulted Carlos, man to man, on the possibility of going up into the mountains to catch a monkey for a pet and asked Guida if she'd ever had a parrot that could talk Portuguese.

Concerning the remarkable view from the top of the Corcovado, however, he was indifferent. While the Almeidas pointed out to Peggy and her family some of the interesting sights 2000 feet below, he raced around the base of the towering statue of Christ, holding his head back at a precarious angle, so that he could see the top.

Then he announced, for the edification of all English-speaking people within earshot, "It's a lot like the Statue of Liberty."

"How do you know? You've never seen the Statue of Liberty," Peggy chided him.

"I have too, in books."

"He may be right at that," said Carlos. "How big is your statue, Tobey? This one weighs more than 1100 tons."

Tobey whistled appreciatively and backed off to the railing for a better look. "I think it's just beautiful at night, when it's lighted," murmured Mrs. Jamison. "Tobey, be careful, hear? Don't lean back quite so far!"

"There's a curious thing," said Mr. Jamison conversationally. "I understand the statue was lighted for the first time through radiotelegraphy by the scientist Marconi, who was operating from his yacht in Italy. Back in the 1930's sometime. Must have been quite a stunt."

"Daddy comes up with the most astonishing facts," put in Peggy, in an effort to explain her parent to Carlos and Guida. "He's the kind of person who reads a lot and remembers things."

Mr. Jamison looked at his daughter pensively. "Do I take that as a compliment or as a rebuke?" he asked, but Peggy was spared the necessity of an answer by her younger brother, who at that moment began to tug at his father's jacket. "I'm hungry," he announced, in a familiar cry of pain. "When do we eat?"

Mrs. Jamison put a finger to her lips, cautioning, "Sh! Don't be rude, dear." But her husband just laughed. "I'm hungry, too. If everybody has oh'd and ah'd enough, let's go."

Lunch proved to be a pleasant interlude. It gave the Jamisons a chance to get better acquainted with their young guests, and bolstered Peggy's morale. The day was going far better than she had expected, and her parents no longer seemed quite so gauche or unattractive. In fact, her mother appeared exactly what she was—sweet and gentle and fashionably ladylike— while her father seemed to be getting along famously with Carlos, in spite of the fact that the Brazilian boy unfailingly addressed him as "sir."

When the party came out of the restaurant Tobey crowded into the front seat of the four-door car between his parents, while Peggy and the Almeidas climbed into the back. The road down the mountain was winding but well-paved, and Mr. Jamison announced that he was glad he'd managed to get a car with a standard gearshift, because he felt safer in second when he was going down a steep grade.

At every twist a fresh panorama was spread before the sight-seers, and Peggy was dividing her attention between the view and Guida's description of how the concrete blocks to build the Christ were hauled up the mountain, when suddenly a trio of boys on bicycles whizzed past, followed by a laggard fourth who seemed to be having trouble with his front wheel.

Utterly without warning, his bicycle hit a stone, skidded, and crashed to the ground, while the lad went flying over the handle bars.

Mr. Jamison jammed on his brakes, throwing all of his passengers forward with a nasty jolt, but in spite of his speed in reacting, the car ploughed into the overturned bicycle with an angry crunch.

"The child!" Mrs. Jamison gasped, because she couldn't see over the hood, and at the same instant her husband pulled on the emergency handle and opened the front door.

But Carlos was even quicker. While Peggy and Guida were pushing themselves back on the seat, from which they had been so unceremoniously dumped, Carlos had managed to get out to the road and around to the front of the car. He gave the wrecked bicycle scarcely a glance. It was the boy to whom he ran, a youngster in his early teens whose head had hit the pavement with an impact that had been actually audible.

When Peggy could see what was happening, she found that the boy was lying in the road like a limp bundle of old clothes. Carlos was on his knees bending over him, while her father was uncertainly feeling his pulse.

Somehow she and Guida managed to tumble out of the car on one side, while her mother and Tobey got out on the other. Shaken and scared, they gathered in a little huddle beside the road, and for once Tobey was speechless with consternation. He didn't even utter the question uppermost in everyone's mind, "Is he badly hurt? Is he—dead?"

As though he was himself anxious to relieve their

minds the boy stirred, then managed to sit up, but he didn't make a move to touch the egg-shaped lump already arising on his forehead. Instead, he gave a shuddering sigh, and a spasm of pain crossed his face. His eyes opened, shut, then opened again in startled terror, and Peggy could hear him whimper a word or two in Portuguese.

"What's he saying?" she asked Guida, abrupt because of her concern.

"It's his arm," Carlos answered for his sister. With his back turned to the girls he seemed to be feeling the wrist, then working his way up to the elbow. At last he raised his eyes to Mr. Jamison's. "I think it must be broken, sir."

"Oh, goodness," murmured Peggy's mother in distress, "what should we do?"

Carlos didn't answer. He stood up, ignoring the injured boy, who was now beginning to cry, and scanned the margins of the hilly road until his eye lit on a broken board fence shoring up an embankment.

While Peggy watched, uncomprehending at first, then deeply interested, he ran to the fence, ripped off a lath about a foot long, and hurried back toward the group around the boy. "Hold this, please," he said to the nearest bystander, who happened to be Guida. With astonishing alacrity, he took off his jacket, untied his tie, and ripped off his shirt. It was the work of only a few seconds to tear the cloth with his teeth and split it into strips. Then he got down on his knees once more and competently braced the injured arm with an amateur splint.

Meanwhile, cars had piled up behind the scene of the accident, and a cab driver had come forward to speak to Mr. Jamison. He was a middle-aged, intelligent-looking fellow, obviously anxious to be of help, but unfortunately he couldn't understand the halting Portuguese in which Peggy's father managed to reply.

Although Carlos seemed to be intent on his ministrations, he spoke up unexpectedly. "I think we'd better take this boy to a hospital, sir. Would it be a good idea to send Mrs. Jamison and the others home in a taxi?"

"Of course, of course. A very good idea." Without any question of Carlos' right to take charge, Mr. Jamison hastened to comply. Peggy, Guida, and Mrs. Jamison were tucked summarily away in the back of an ancient sedan, with Tobey riding up beside the driver as usual. "Aw, jeepers," he kept protesting for the next five minutes, "I don't see why I couldn't have gone with the *men*."

Peggy, still shaken, said, "Oh, Tobey, shut up," and her mother fretted, "Please, children, don't quarrel." Guida sat without saying anything until they reached level ground once more, then sighed in belated relief. "That *criança* was lucky not to be killed. A second or two *mais ou menos—*"

Suddenly they were all discussing the accident at once. "Carlos was simply marvelous!" Peggy cried softly. "Where did he ever learn to make a splint like that?"

"Your father was marvelous, too," Guida told her, instead of replying. "He was so quick to stop!"

"They were both simply wonderful," put in Mrs. Jamison, who was inclined to gush in times of stress. "I don't know what we'd all have done if we'd been alone." She drew a tremendous breath and added, "I'm not sure whether I'll ever get up courage to drive in this town, I declare."

Peggy was seized by a fit of nervous giggles, the aftermath of strain. "Whenever Mother gets excited she goes all moonlight-and-magnolias," she murmured to Guida.

"Hush—I do not!" protested Mrs. Jamison, as indignant as a schoolgirl, but her very accent disproved her words, and she found herself joining the momentary amusement at her own expense.

Back in the apartment, Jacinta was told the story piecemeal. "What you all need is a cup of tea," said the Bahian woman promptly. "Now just sit down and relax, and I'll brew some right up."

"That's what comes of having a maid who has worked for Baptist missionaries," said Mrs. Jamison thankfully, when Jacinta had left the room. "Tea can be a mighty comforting beverage."

If Guida would have preferred a *cafèzinho,* she was too well-bred to mention it. Instead, she made polite conversation with her hostess, concealing the anxiety with which they were all awaiting Mr. Jamison's and

Carlos' return. "Peggy tells me you come from a city in Alabama that has a Carnival something like ours—Mobile, isn't it?"

Mrs. Jamison nodded in the manner of a woman always pleased to discuss her home town. "On Shrove Tuesday. But of course our celebration is small, compared with New Orleans or Rio. I understand that here all business stops for three days."

"That's right." Guida turned to Peggy. "Even the schools close," she added with a grin.

But Mrs. Jamison scarcely heard her. She was looking back into the past. "I can remember watching the floats go past the Athelstan Club stand when I was about your age, or maybe even younger. There was one made up of huge gaudy papier-mâché snakes, and another just massed with azaleas. Mobile is famous for its azaleas, you know."

Guida obviously did not know, but she continued to be polite. "I'm sure it must be a lovely city."

"Oh, not like Rio. There's no doubt about it, Rio is unique," replied Peggy's mother. "But there are still some wonderful old grilled-iron galleries, and there's lots of faded brick, and on summer nights the Spanish moss almost hides the moon on Mobile Bay." She turned to greet the arrival of the tea tray. "Thank you, Jacinta."

Peggy got up to serve Guida, and brought the conversation back to the present with a query addressed to no one in particular. "I wonder how long they'll be?"

Guida glanced at her wrist watch. "A while longer, I should think. They'll need to make arrangements for the arm to be set, and get in touch with the boy's parents."

"I can't get over how *efficient* Carlos was!" put in Peggy. "He must have taken a first-aid course or something at school."

"No," Guida said, "no." She seemed to be pondering the question of her brother's skill as she raised her cup and cautiously sipped the hot tea. "We have an uncle who is a doctor," she told the Jamisons, "and both Carlos and I usually work in the clinic summers. Mama thinks it is good for us to know something about life in the *favelas*, you see."

"The *favelas*?" questioned Peggy.

"A *favela* is a slum," Guida explained. "You've noticed those huddles of packing-box shanties that climb the mountainsides."

"Oh yes! They look rather picturesque," Mrs. Jamison observed.

A reproachful expression, quickly veiled, crossed Guida's bright eyes. "I'm afraid they're only picturesque from a distance. The poor people are so ignorant. . . ." Her voice trailed off, as though it was a subject too painful to discuss. "Maybe you'd like to help out sometime, Peggy, over the holidays. My uncle never has enough assistants."

The suggestion didn't sound in the least appealing, but Peggy was genuinely fond of Guida and she didn't want to offend her. "Maybe," she replied vaguely, and glanced at her mother. "I'm not very good around sick people, actually, and I can't stand the sight of blood."

At that moment the hall door burst open, and in came Mr. Jamison and Carlos, looking remarkably jaunty and pleased with themselves. Mrs. Jamison got to her feet with a welcoming smile. "Oh, good! We didn't expect you for hours!"

"Everything is under control," Peggy's father said at once. "We found a surgeon on duty who could set the arm, and the boy's parents came at once. There's nothing to worry about, nothing at all, but it certainly was a stroke of luck the bicycle didn't throw the lad under our wheels."

"You bet it was!" seconded Carlos, whose jacket was draped nonchalantly over his bare brown shoulders and whose eyes were shining with controlled excitement. "It was a clean break, the doctor said, a simple fracture. The easiest kind of all to set."

"The doctor also said that Carlos did a fine job of emergency first aid," added Mr. Jamison. "And let me tell you, I'm plenty grateful. Without that temporary splint our young friend would have been a pretty unhappy boy."

Carlos made a deprecating gesture, but Mr. Jamison laid an affectionate hand on his shoulder. "Don't be modest. You did a bang-up job!"

After the Almeidas had left he enlarged on this observation. "Carlos and I got pretty well acquainted," he told Peggy. "He's a very interesting young man."

It was the first time her father had ever dignified

one of her beaux by any other term than "boy," so Peggy could scarcely hide her surprise. "In what way?" she asked.

"He's not one of these drifters," her father said. "He knows what he wants to do."

"And what's that?"

"He's going to study to be a doctor," Mr. Jamison said. "He wants to take his degree in the United States, then come back here and work on tropical diseases. Seems he has an uncle who has fired his enthusiasm for what can be accomplished right here in Rio." He glanced from his daughter to his wife and commented, "It's good to see a Brazilian lad interested in a service career."

Peggy, although she made no comment, felt a prick of chagrin that her father should have discovered something about Carlos that she hadn't suspected. A doctor—well! Suddenly it seemed the ideal profession, to be accepted as an integral part of his personality. Dr. Carlos Almeida. How dignified the engraved name would look on a polished brass plate, attached to an office door.

A doctor's wife, however, was said to have a lonely life. She thought of Mrs. Bishop, a friend of her parents', who was always late for dinner parties because "the doctor" had been detained. And there were many unfortunate times when her husband didn't show up at all.

But Peggy shrugged off any sympathy for Mrs. Bishop, a pallid woman, with no instinct for the dramatic. As for herself, she would make of her husband a heroic figure, working to the point of exhaustion, curing the ills of the world, with only a passing thought of regret for a social engagement missed. She, Peggy. . . .

"What are you daydreaming about, darling?" Mrs. Jamison asked.

"Me?" Peggy looked up with a start, compelled to fabricate an answer that sounded reasonable. "I was just thinking," she replied after a moment, "that maybe I ought to look into this clinic thing that Guida mentioned. Two and a half months can be an awfully long vacation, unless you have something interesting to do."

Chapter 6

The shared experience of Independence Day put Peggy's acquaintanceship with Guida Almeida on an entirely new basis, which finally slipped over into the friendship she had bragged about—prematurely—to Laurette King.

"You're lucky," Becky told Peggy frankly one afternoon, "to have made friends with a Brazilian family so fast. Usually it takes ages to be really accepted. The Cariocas are pleasant and everything, but we're outsiders, after all."

It was mid-October, and Peggy and Becky were staying after school to do some research on a biology paper. The library was all but deserted; the girls were tired of making notes from reference books, and they were leaning on their elbows and gossiping companionably.

"Guida and I got along from the moment we met. We just liked one another—I don't know why exactly," Peggy mused.

"That goes for Carlos too, doesn't it?" Becky asked mischievously.

"Don't tease me," Peggy begged. "Carlos is something special. I've never met anybody like him. He's gay and fun and perfectly gorgeous looking, and yet he has a very serious side. You know something, Becky, I wouldn't be surprised if he became a really great man!"

"Wow," exclaimed Becky inelegantly. "You really have got it bad!"

Peggy slapped a book shut. "I *said* please don't tease me!"

"All right, all right. Take it easy." Becky's grin was an apology, and she switched her approach to the subject. "What does Guida think of you and Carlos? Is it awkward at all?"

"Not in the least," said Peggy honestly. "I think Guida is sort of amused, especially because Cleo is so green with envy whenever Carlos pays me a bit of attention."

"Now you're being coy. You know perfectly well he pays you a great deal of attention, and that Cleo has every right to be burned to a crisp."

"I don't see why."

"Oh, Peggy, don't be naïve. Until you came along Dom Carlos was her exclusive property. You can't expect her to be overjoyed when a foreigner walks in and takes over"—Becky snapped her fingers—"just like that!"

Peggy frowned. There was something wrong with

this conversation. It was too superficial. The way she felt about Carlos Almeida was something she didn't want to discuss with Becky or anyone else. She wished she had never mentioned Cleo, because jealousy was an ugly emotion from which she herself was not entirely exempt.

It swept her now, impelling her to say, "Cleo still sees plenty of Carlos. The families are great friends, and they have Sunday lunch together all the time."

What Peggy did not admit, either then or later, was that she begrudged Cleo those Sunday lunches only because *she* had never been invited to the Almeida house. Both Guida and Carlos came frequently to the apartment on Avenida Atlântica, and whenever there was an outing afoot Peggy was included in the plans. She met the Almeidas by prearrangement, on the beach, at the tennis courts, at basketball games, anywhere that a crowd was gathered, but it apparently never occurred to the young Brazilians that they might reciprocate the Jamisons' hospitality. North Americans were not introduced casually into a Brazilian home. This demanded a great occasion.

The occasion came at the end of the second quarter, after report cards had come out and Peggy had discovered that her grades were adequate, if not brilliant.

"My birthday is December first," Guida said to Peggy one Saturday morning when they were decorating the gym for a sophomore dance. "I'm going to have a party and I hope you can come."

"I'd love to!" Peggy was both pleased and surprised.

"You'll get a proper invitation," Guida promised, "but I just thought I'd mention it, so you'd be sure to save the date."

"Is it to be a very big party?" asked Peggy from the top of a stepladder, where she was attaching bright-colored paper flags—a prop used for all Brazilian *festas*—to a netting canopy.

"Yes. You see it's a very special birthday. I'll be fifteen."

"*Fifteen?*" Astonished, Peggy almost lost her balance. "You mean you've been fourteen all along? Why, Guida, I never dreamed! I thought you were my age at least!"

Guida smiled, quite unembarrassed. "I guess Brazilian girls look older. Besides, of course, I'm a little ahead of where I should be in school."

"I'll say you are," murmured Peggy. "I knew you were bright, but I didn't know you were that bright!" She looked down with new respect at the slight alert-eyed girl, who was unrolling a fresh batch of flags at the foot of the ladder; yet she knew that it was more than just schoolbook cleverness that made Guida seem older. In comparison to any fourteen- or fifteen-year-old back home in Charlotte, Guida was incredibly mature.

"A fifteenth birthday party here is something like a debut in the United States," the Brazilian girl explained. "In the old days it used to mean that a girl had reached the marriageable age, so the family held a big celebration to launch her in society. Now, of course, we marry a little later, but the parties are much the same."

The coming dance, to which Peggy had been looking forward only mildly, because senior boys were not invited to sophomore affairs, became eclipsed entirely by the realization that at last she had won Guida's complete acceptance. By now Peggy knew enough of Brazilian social customs to understand that her inclusion on the guest list was an honor. The decision must have been made in a family conference, not by Guida alone.

Peggy could scarcely wait to get home for lunch and tell her mother. A dozen questions needed to be answered. What sort of dress would be required? Was it customary to take a birthday present? Or perhaps, this being Brazil, flowers should be sent in advance. Peggy, by now, was aware that her mother seemed to receive and give orchids or roses on all sorts of improbable occasions.

She broke away from the decorating job in the gym as soon as it was decently possible and hurried home, only to find the apartment empty except for Jacinta, who said that her mother and Tobey had not come up from the beach.

The noon sun was hot, and there was little or no breeze, so Peggy decided to change into a bathing suit and go for a swim too. Arriving on the beach five minutes later, she found her mother swimming systematically in the calm water beyond the breakers, on a stint that was supposed to be good for a waistline thickened by South American starches and sweets.

Peggy dove through the waves and swam out. "Guess what!" she said, when she came within earshot. "Guida's having a sort of coming-out party, and I'm invited."

"How nice," Mrs. Jamison said rather lazily.

"It's important," Peggy insisted. "I may be the only North American there. Besides, I've never been to the Almeidas, you know."

"That's right." Mrs. Jamison turned over and floated on her back. "It's high time they asked you, actually."

Any criticism of her friends made Peggy prickle with annoyance. "Oh, Mother, don't be obtuse!" she scolded. "I'm new here. Brazilians are different. Our families have never met. There are all sorts of reasons why they've waited. I'm just glad to be invited at all. And I think it will be terribly interesting!"

"Of course it will, dear," said Mrs. Jamison soothingly. "And I like the young Almeidas very much—they have such lovely manners—but in Charlotte, if you had new friends, well—I'd call on their mother. It would be only proper. You know that."

Peggy felt ages old. "It isn't the custom here," she explained patiently. "Senhora Almeida could never call on you. She'd have to be introduced by some mutual friend or something, and we don't have any mutual friends." Suddenly she wanted to drop the subject. "Are you almost ready to go in, Mother? I'm starved."

Mrs. Jamison turned and headed toward shore. "You

sound like Tobey," she called to her daughter. "Which reminds me, we have to collect Tobey. He's building a fort."

The fort was something of a masterpiece, as sand architecture goes. It was big and thick-walled and had turrets, mounted with imaginative flags made from paper napkins. Tobey and a trio of his beach pals were so intent on the finishing touches that Mrs. Jamison had to tap her son on the shoulder before he became aware of her presence.

Both Peggy and her mother made sure to be duly admiring. The other boys, two of them dark and crinkly-haired with big shy smiles, the other fair and chubby with a German cast to his features, stood aside and listened to their unintelligible English comments, exchanging glances of mute amusement at such gibberish.

"Lunch in half an hour," Mrs. Jamison reminded her son when she turned to leave. She nodded impartially to the other boys, but as they crossed the sand she murmured to Peggy, "I do wish Tobey wouldn't spend all his time with those darkies, even if they are in the same room at school. There must be other boys he can find for friends."

Peggy wasn't surprised by her mother's concern, but she thought it was unjustified. "I don't think it matters down here," she replied.

"Well, I do," her mother said firmly. "Tobey's at a very impressionable age."

A residue of her earlier annoyance led Peggy to ask

flippantly, "So what? He finds out black boys can be fun to play with as well as white boys. Is that so up-setting?"

Mrs. Jamison frowned. "I was talking about *friends*."

Peggy sighed. "Sometimes you're frightfully old-fashioned, Mother. After all, he doesn't bring them to the *house*."

"But he might," retorted Mrs. Jamison. "He actually might. I don't think he even *sees* the difference in the color of their skins."

"And isn't that good?" Peggy asked, feeling forward-looking and superior, although up until this very min-ute she had always accepted her mother's viewpoint. "Isn't that pretty basically what the world needs—a new generation that can't see the difference? I think we ought to be pleased that Tobey chooses boys he likes for his friends, regardless of the fact that they're white, black, or sky-blue pink."

"Now you're talking foolishness, Margaret, and you know it." (Mrs. Jamison never called her daughter Margaret unless she was extraordinarily serious.) "It's all very well to talk that way in a country where there's little or no color line, but we're not going to be in Rio forever. And I've got to see that when we go back to Charlotte Tobey doesn't take up with all kinds of trash."

Peggy was becoming more and more indignant. "Mother, those boys aren't trashy. They're perfectly respectable. They go to Tobey's school and they prob-ably come from very nice folks. You're being—" She

sought for a word she had seen in Charlotte news-
papers when the segregation problem was under discussion. "You're being reactionary."

"Who's being reactionary?" asked Mr. Jamison, as
he opened the apartment door and overheard the last
word.

"Mother," said Peggy bluntly. "She's living in the
past. Just because Tobey's playing with a couple of
little colored boys on the beach—"

"It isn't just because of that," interrupted Mrs. Jamison. "I was talking about something that could be a
problem, that's all."

A troubled expression replaced the welcome in Mr.
Jamison's eyes, and Peggy became aware that she had
touched a tender spot in the understanding that existed
between her parents. The difference in their New York
and Alabama backgrounds had inevitably bred different points of view on the question of color, and they
usually found it sensible to avoid any discussion that
would lead to argument.

Now, in her own maturing wisdom, Peggy made a
genuine effort to stifle her irritation and talk about
something else. In this her mother abetted her, because it would never do to offend Jacinta, should she
overhear. As Peggy changed into a sleeveless cotton
shirt and skirt, she decided that this instinctive protection of another's feelings was as much a part of
her mother's breeding as her concern about Tobey's
companions. She was a darling, compared to most

mothers, and Peggy adored her. If only she didn't
seem so stuffy every once in a while!

Yet how could she help it? An upper-class white
girl, born in Mobile or in any one of a hundred other
Southern towns, where the streets were lined with live
oaks heavy with Spanish moss, was raised by very
definite standards. Peggy could imagine the taboos
learned by the young Virginia Cullen, the walls
thrown up against change, which Southerners naturally dreaded. Virginia had been taught to be courteous
to everyone, including Negroes, as long as they kept
their place. She had been taught, not formally but by
example, the correct modulation of voice, words, feelings, with which a well-bred person should treat people whose skin was colored differently from her own.

She had learned her lesson well, yet she got along
splendidly with servants, including Jacinta, as Peggy
had to admit. Colored people liked to work for Mrs.
Jamison. She was gentle, fair, even a little indulgent,
because usually she grew to love the people who
worked for her, just as, in a vague, almost wistful way,
she loved lace and sunsets and flowers.

And she had taught Peggy her own code of conduct. As she stood in front of her mirror readying herself for lunch, Peggy could remember almost every
tenet. Never use the word "nigger." Always shake
hands with old Negro friends. It isn't "correct" to call
a colored man "mister," invite him into the living
room, or sit with him on a bench in the park. And al-

ways, always, be on the alert for a Negro who doesn't conform; he may be dangerous!

That's the trouble now, Peggy thought as she dabbed her nose with powder. Mother's afraid, afraid for Tobey in a little way, but afraid for herself and the things she stands for in a bigger way. She doesn't know what to make of the situation down here, so it frightens her.

Having rearranged her thoughts in a pattern of compassion and understanding, Peggy went in to lunch. She told her father about Guida's coming birthday party, complimented Tobey again on his wonderful sand fort, and generally acted so adult and restrained that her mother looked at her rather anxiously, and asked if she was feeling ill.

Chapter 7

As Peggy had suspected, she was the only one of Guida's North American school friends to be invited to the birthday party. The formal invitation was delivered to the apartment "by hand," in the manner by which many Rio residents evaded the uncertainties of the postal system. In simple Portuguese, which she could now read with ease, Peggy was asked to be present at eight o'clock on Friday evening, December 1.

About protocol she consulted Becky. "Have you ever been to a Brazilian girl's fifteenth birthday party?"

"Yes, once," Becky said reassuringly. "What do you want to know?"

"Do you take a present?"

"By all means."

"What sort of present, exactly?"

"Oh, a book, a bottle of perfume, a record. The usual thing. Some of the boys may bring flowers," Becky added, "but I wouldn't, if I were you."

Peggy giggled. "I see what you mean. Guida and I aren't going steady, after all."

It was to Cleo Andrade that she turned when it came to the question of clothes. Becky, she felt, might not be completely reliable in this respect. She needed a Brazilian point of view.

Peggy found it a trifle awkward to approach Cleo, even though they often found themselves at the same table at lunch. She felt as though she should be waving a white flag of truce as she asked tentatively, "Will Guida's birthday party be very dressy, do you think?"

"Are you invited?" Cleo couldn't conceal her surprise, but she quickly turned tactful. "Of course! I forgot for a moment about you two girls."

There was something about the phrasing that made Cleo sound older, superior, yet Peggy swallowed her pride and plunged ahead. "I really need some help on what to wear."

Cleo shrugged. "Party clothes. Something pretty but not too bare. There will be a great many relatives and very close family friends."

This information managed to sound so terrifying that Peggy's excitement gave way to trepidation. Would they all talk Portuguese? And even if a good many of the young people spoke English, would they bother to include her, or would she be alone and uncomfortable?

With a conscious effort, she preserved her appearance of aplomb in front of Cleo, but to her mother she confided her fear and uncertainty. "Maybe I'd better not try to go," she worried. "Maybe I'd better send regrets."

"Nonsense. If Guida has invited you she'll take care of you and make sure you have a good time. Besides, Carlos will be there."

The mere mention of Carlos gave Peggy courage, and she returned to her original concern. "But what can I wear?"

There was a conspicuous difference between the way Brazilian girls and those from the States dressed and wore their hair. Peggy had heard it said that it was considered a disgrace in Rio for a mother to dress better than her daughter, and it was certain that girls here were more clothes-conscious than they were back home. Hair was teased into the latest fashion, skirts were tighter and more extreme in cut, and the Paris fashion magazines were followed by the well to do with a slavishness that perplexed the more casual North Americans.

"You have plenty of things to wear," said Mrs. Jamison, after giving the matter some thought. "What about the dress with the nasturtium print?"

"That's so *bright*," objected Peggy.

"Your sleeveless black linen, then?"

"Not *black!*"

Finally they settled on a beige, Chinese-silk frock, with intricate little frogs clasping a narrow belt above a fullish skirt. Peggy was sure it made her look too young, but her mother insisted it would be perfect for the occasion, and when she was finally dressed for the party she had to admit that her tanned skin and burnt-orange hair were made more effective by the pale, soft fabric. Bearing a prettily wrapped bottle of "Ballerina" and a carefully chosen birthday card, she set off at eight-thirty with her father for the Almeidas' house.

To arrive at a party a half hour or more after the stated time was a Brazilian convention that exasperated Mr. Jamison, who was a punctual sort. He grumbled that he didn't approve of young girls staying up until midnight or later and said that he intended to call for his daughter at eleven-thirty sharp.

"But things will be just getting *started,*" wailed Peggy. "Becky says at the party she went to nobody went home until one o'clock!"

Finally they compromised on midnight, although Peggy didn't consider it a compromise but a defeat. She thanked her father icily and slammed the car door a little louder than necessary when he dropped her in front of a grilled-iron gate, leading to a brightly lighted house.

Then, as the car pulled away, she had a mad impulse to run shouting after it. Never in her life had she felt so alone, not even on her first day at dancing class. She wished suddenly and desperately that she had decided not to come. But a servant, standing in the doorway, had seen her at the open gate, and there was nothing to do but go in.

The house was much larger than she had expected. Chandeliers glinted on the black-and-white marble floor of a square entrance hall, beyond which double doors opened to a leafy garden. At the right a curving staircase with a polished brass railing led to an upper floor.

As Peggy hesitated the servant murmured something in Portuguese, which she took to be the equivalent of "Right upstairs, Miss." She nodded, smiled, and with as light a step as she could muster crossed the hall and started to climb the stairs.

Then she breathed a sigh of relief. There at the top was Guida, in a slim white dress. The moment she saw Peggy she gave a cry of pleasure and turned from talking with an elderly gentleman to come part way down the stairs.

"How nice! I want you to meet my mother." Guida drew Peggy toward a slender, stately woman, who turned with a warm smile. "This is my friend Margaret Jamison," Guida said.

Peggy found her hand clasped strongly. "My dear—Guida has been telling us such nice things about you, so I'm especially happy that at last we meet."

A trifle awkwardly, because she was busy gathering first impressions of eyes like Carlos', upswept dark hair, a simple black dress, and a husky voice, Peggy said, "I've been anxious to meet you, too, Mrs.—I mean Senhora—Almeida."

The Brazilian woman patted Peggy's hand and laughed gently. "You must call me Dona Plácida. Here we are apt to ignore the surname, you see."

"Dona Plácida," murmured Peggy obediently. It sounded like water running in a brook.

A moment later her hostess turned away to greet other new arrivals and Peggy was left with Guida. "Happy birthday," she said conventionally, and held out the little package she had brought.

"How sweet of you!" cried Guida, her eyes as lively as mercury. She ripped off the paper wrapping and crumpled it, then exclaimed over the perfume. " 'Ballerina'—I've never used it. What fun!"

She put the perfume on a side table with some other presents, while Peggy scanned the rooms opening off the hall for a familiar face. To her right was a living room leading to a balcony, and to her left was a dining room, at the far end of which a long refreshment table had been set up.

The early arrivals, who were standing in little groups chatting in Portuguese, were mostly older people—Cleo's promised relatives of the Almeidas', Peggy surmised. A couple of Carlos' Brazilian classmates were standing on the balcony with glasses in their hands, but although she knew them to speak to, Peggy could scarcely cross the room and deliberately seek them out.

Again she was swept by the unaccustomed feeling of panic, which had attacked her at the gate. Then she felt a hand on her arm and turned with a start to look up into Carlos' smiling face.

"Hi there, Peggy. You look almost as scared as you did that first day in the school cafeteria."

Peggy swallowed hard and managed a reciprocal smile. "You always seem to come to my rescue at exactly the right time."

"Just call me Lancelot," Carlos teased. "Have you met Mama and Papa yet?"

"Guida introduced me to your mother," Peggy replied. "I've just arrived."

"Then I'll take you around and see that you meet some of our guests," Carlos proposed. "At the moment they're mostly cousins and uncles and aunts, but the younger crowd will be coming along any time now."

"I was afraid I'd be early," Peggy fretted.

"You're not a bit early. It's just that everybody else is late."

They laughed at this sally together, and again, as on many a previous occasion, everything became easy. Peggy's eyes began to sparkle, her hair seemed to take on shine, and she started to feel as vivid and attractive as Carlos obviously found her. In other words, she relaxed.

Going from group to group under the aegis of Guida's brother was quite different from braving a roomful of strangers on her own. The Brazilians, many of whom could speak quite adequate English, graciously switched to the foreign language as soon as Peggy appeared. Those who were more limited linguists assumed that she could speak French, but before her lack could become embarrassing, Carlos cleverly whisked her on. As the rooms began to fill, the older people automatically separated themselves from the young guests, most of the adults congregating in the dining room, where wine, beer, and Brazilian *batida* were being served.

At a bar set up on the balcony off the living room, Guida's friends were finding Coca-Cola, *guaraná*, and silver dishes full of salty tidbits which Carlos called *salgadinhos*. The parquet floor in the big hall had been waxed for dancing, and at nine-thirty Guida was officially presented to society by the pleasant custom of giving her father the first dance.

People were still coming in—aunts, uncles, godparents, cousins, friends of all ages—everyone coming to give Guida an *abraço*, the affectionate Brazilian embrace. Those who hadn't sent flowers on ahead brought gifts, and as the evening wore on and each gift was opened and exclaimed over prettily by the honored one, she became more and more radiant.

For Peggy the party began to take on a kaleidoscopic quality. One moment she was making polite conversation with an eighty-year-old gentleman leaning on a cane, the next she was doing a samba with a Brazilian lad, who was studying physics at the University of Brazil. Carlos, who had gone off to pursue his duties as host, had not yet danced with her, but on the other hand she was not lacking for partners, and on the floor all language difficulties disappeared.

Peggy was a good dancer. She had a natural sense of rhythm and the easy co-ordination common to American girls. But she had something more, a zest more typical of Brazilians than of their counterparts in the United States. Within a very short time it became obvious that she was having a small personal triumph. Everyone wanted to dance with the girl with the copper-colored hair.

It was while she was in the arms of Roberto Santos, whose young wife Josefina was dancing with the university student, that Peggy finally begged for a rest. Immediately, with the usual good manners of a Carioca, Roberto led her from the floor, and the first person they encountered was Cleo Andrade.

Tonight Cleo, in cobalt blue, was as beautiful as an exotic moth. Impulsively, Peggy gasped her admiration. "How lovely you look!"

Cleo acknowledged the compliment politely and introduced Peggy to her parents, with whom she had just arrived. Her mother was a big overblown woman, carefully corseted, and her father was slight and thin and so quick in his movements that he seemed like a fox terrier paired with a great Dane.

Senhor Paulo Andrade squeezed Peggy's hand, then dropped it hastily and said to Roberto, "We've got to find Cleo's young cousin. Have you seen Guida anywhere?"

When they had left, after the exchange of a few pleasantries, Peggy asked, rather as though she was speaking to herself, "Are they really cousins of the Almeidas, then?"

Roberto nodded. "Distant ones—second or third, I believe. So many people in Rio are related to one another that it's hard to remember."

"Of course," Peggy murmured, as though it was of no importance. The university student had just come up with Josefina, and the foursome exchanged partners and started to dance again.

A few minutes later, with a sense of surprise more than shock, Peggy saw Carlos dancing, for the first time that evening, with Cleo. Jealousy twisted through her like a skewer, but she scolded herself with the reminder that Cleo was practically a member of the family, and that she herself was a stranger here. When the record was finished and the dancers came to a halt, Carlos at once led his cousin over to Peggy and partners were again exchanged.

Dancing with Carlos was everything Peggy had imagined. He led her in the most intricate steps with a command to be envied even by an older and more experienced man. Nor did he seem to be concentrating on his technique at the expense of his attention to the girl, whose head reached just an inch above his shoulder. "You should not come, with your beautiful hair, and take all the young men away from our Brazilian girls," he chided, in acknowledgment that he had been watching. "It isn't fair."

"I'm just a novelty," Peggy assured him.

"A novelty that may well become—how do you say it?—a fashion."

"Now you're being terribly Brazilian!" Peggy teased. "Haven't you learned that girls from the States don't know how to respond to compliments? They go all

weak-kneed and say, 'You're kidding!' As, of course,
you are."

"I have never been more sincere," Carlos told her,
then said in a different tone, "Mama's trying to catch
my eye. I think she wants to talk to you."

Peggy didn't have time to wonder why. A second
later she found herself standing, along with Carlos,
in front of Dona Plácida beside the dining-room door.

"Ah, *obrigado*, Carlinhos," the *Senhora* said. "I just
wanted to tell Guida's young friend that we will be
delighted to have her join us at the clinic this coming
summer. You see, Guida has told me you are interested."

Although Peggy had not decided on a definite com-
mitment, she concealed any hesitation. "Oh, I am!"
she said, with sudden decision. "Particularly, Dona
Plácida, if I could come at the same hours you and
Guida would be there."

The approval in Carlos' eyes, when he danced away
with her again, was unmistakable. "I think you're very
generous," he said. "And believe me, the clinic needs
all the volunteer help that's available. Have you met
my uncle, by the way? He's right over there."

Dr. João Vilaça was helping himself to food from the
mesa de doces, a long supper table laden with all
sorts of Brazilian delicacies at one end of the dining
room. The fascinating array of strange and wonderful
dishes was as elaborate as a holiday buffet at the Country Club, and Peggy realized that this fifteenth birthday of Guida's was a special occasion indeed.

She shifted her attention to the bespectacled doctor, whose swarthy yet sallow skin testified to a life spent indoors, and watched him greet his nephew with affection, putting down his plate so that he could embrace him. *"Como vai?"*

"I have a recruit for your clinic, Uncle João. This is Senhorita Margaret Jamison. My uncle, Dr. Vilaça."

"Marvelous!" Dr. Vilaça switched to English immediately. He added with a warm humorousness, "Perhaps I should embrace the *senhorita* too. In any event, I shall be glad to have these two extra hands." He smiled at Peggy and glanced at his nephew inquisitively. "And you, Carlinhos, how much of your time may I count on this coming summer? Three days a week?"

"Something like that," replied Carlos, evading a conclusive answer. "Of course, now that I know that Peggy will be around I'll try to do a little better than last year."

Dr. Vilaça laughed heartily and clapped his nephew on the arm. "A rogue, this one," he said to Peggy with a wink. "Yet I think he may make a good doctor someday, if we can pry him loose from the girls."

There was a minor commotion at the other end of the room, eliminating any need to reply. Peggy turned to see Carlos' father coming in from the hall, with a fragile, ancient lady leaning on his arm. She had a face like a walnut, brown and so full of wrinkles that her eyes seemed to have disappeared into her skull, which was topped by a quantity of woolly white hair, and she reminded Peggy of a Negro preacher who traveled around Charlotte collecting for home missions. The dress she wore, of unseasonably heavy silk crepe, was as brown as her skin, and she walked with the uncertain, hesitant, stiff-kneed step of the very old.

With a murmured, monosyllabic apology, Carlos hurried across the room to find a chair for the little creature, and Peggy found herself alone with the doctor. He answered her unspoken question. "That's Dona Virgilia, my brother-in-law's mother—Carlos' grandmother."

"But—" But she's a Negro, Peggy almost said aloud, so clamorous was her realization of this incredible fact. Beside her, Dr. Vilaça said quietly, "Yes, she's very dark. She was born on a sugar plantation in Bahia, you see."

Peggy was too dumfounded to answer, and stood staring with such an utter loss of poise that she scarcely realized Carlos was back at her side. "They're going to cut the cake in a few minutes," he said. "But first we'll all sing 'Parabéns.' It's the custom here—a Brazilian version of 'Happy birthday to you.'"

A white-jacketed waiter, bearing a big white birthday cake, elaborately frosted and lighted with fifteen flickering candles, appeared through a side door and placed his trophy squarely in the center of the long buffet. There was a transient silence, then a round of applause, and immediately the company burst into song:

> Parabéns a você
> Nesta data querida
> Muitas felicidades
> Muitos anos de vida.

Guida stepped forward and blew out the candles just as the clock struck midnight, and a moment later a servant appeared, looking for a foreigner with red hair. "Senhorita Margaret Jamison?" he inquired, stumbling over the unfamiliar name. Peggy nodded, said polite good-by's to the Almeidas, and walked as though in a trance to join her father, who was waiting —prompt as usual—in the hall downstairs.

Chapter 8

On the way home Peggy was abnormally quiet.

"Did you have a good time?" her father asked conversationally, as they walked out to the car.

"Yes, very."

"Looked like a big crowd."

"It was." With a conscious effort she added, "Lots of relatives."

It didn't occur to her that she sounded sulky rather than distracted, and that her father would misinterpret her noncommittal replies, believing them to be induced by annoyance at being called for too early. She sat huddled in the corner of the seat, her eyes wide open, staring at the lights along the boulevard without seeing them, her father never guessing that she was relieved to get away.

In the elevator she yawned with deliberate intent, and instead of hurrying to sit on the foot of her mother's bed and tell her all about the party, she paused for barely a moment in the bedroom doorway. "I'm sleepy," she fibbed, after saying, "yes, it was

107

lovely. Lots of fun." She yawned again. "Let's talk about it in the morning, h'm?"

Alone at last, Peggy undressed automatically, hanging her dress in the closet and folding her underwear on the back of a chair with unaccustomed carefulness. She slipped between the cool sheets gratefully, but she didn't snuggle down against the pillow. Instead, she sat on the end of her spine with her neck pushed uncomfortably against the headboard, trying to sort out emotions she hadn't known she possessed.

Like dice dancing against one another in a cardboard cup, words jangled in her mind—words on the signs over doors in railroad and bus stations, over drinking fountains, over theater entrances.

White . . . Colored . . . White . . . Colored . . .

Clenching her hands, Peggy also belligerently clenched her teeth. She wasn't going to give Carlos up! She liked him better than any other boy she had ever known, and she knew the liking wasn't superficial. He was a very special person, with a serious side as well as a gay one. He was sympathetic, he was kind, he was altogether wonderful!

Besides, in Brazil the color of a person's skin didn't matter. Daddy had said so. Here there was no invisible line cutting Rio into segments, as the South was cut. Here there was no white town, no colored town, no problem about a family like Ella's. . . .

Peggy hadn't thought about Ella for years, but now she could see her quite clearly, coming down the steps of the little frame house by the grade crossing, her light-brown curls bobbing in the sun, her gray eyes as trusting as a baby spaniel's. She had a book in her hand, a book about a horse named Misty, which Peggy had loaned her a week before. "I loved it," she cried. "I just loved it. Thank you so much!"

Peggy's mother, waiting in the car, had looked strangely troubled. "How did you get to know that child?" she asked.

Peggy couldn't remember. "I don't know, but I like her. She's nice."

Very clearly, as though it were yesterday, she remembered her mother's next remark. "I don't think you'd better play with her any more, dear. She's colored, you see."

"Colored? But she's as white as I am!"

"Please don't argue," her mother had said. "I know the family. Her sister is the Leona who works for the Fosters. Now do you understand?"

No, Peggy thought, she hadn't understood, not until this very minute. But now she knew why her mother's voice had been sharp that day, while her face had been sad and uncertain. Although Ella had been white, Leona had been dark—as dark, almost, as Carlos' grandmother.

Words again—senseless words—began to beat on Peggy's mind like jungle drums. . . .

Darkie . . . uppity . . . sinful . . . tradition. . . .

Guilt began to encircle her like a tangible thing, while she pushed to the back of her mind other words she seldom heard and never used—bad words, buried deep in the past. Peggy twitched her shoulders and frowned at the tricks her own subconscious was playing. These words had nothing to do with her, or with Brazil.

Hadn't she, just the other day, criticized her mother for being reactionary? Very well, this was a chance to prove her own broad-mindedness. In Brazil it was no sin to have a Negro grandmother.

Besides, she needn't tell.

Guilt again—a new personal feeling of guilt—swept over Peggy. Why shouldn't she tell, actually? She was bad at keeping secrets, especially from her mother. And after all, if she believed what she professed—

Anyway, how did she know Carlos' grandmother wasn't just a very dark Portuguese? Maybe she had been wrong to jump to such a quick conclusion. But the little lady's unmistakable African features taunted her. You're just making excuses and you know it, Margaret Cullen Jamison!

Peggy slept fitfully, but when she awakened, one thing at least was settled. She knew that this was one secret she intended to keep. At breakfast she managed to talk gaily of the party, describing the Almeida house, the dancing, the refreshments, and the Portuguese words sung to the tune of "Happy Birthday." She told her family about Carlos' uncle, the doctor, and announced that she had promised Dona Plácida to work in the clinic when school closed, if she could get permission.

"You wouldn't mind, would you?" she asked.

Mrs. Jamison looked hesitant. "I suppose not." She turned to her husband. "Unless you think it might actually be dangerous. I mean the germs—"

Mr. Jamison laughed. "Peggy's a good, strong, husky girl," he replied. "And by summer she should be pretty acclimated to the Brazilian bugs."

It still startled Peggy to hear the vacation, which would start December 16 and end February 26, called "summer," yet with each passing day the weather was getting warmer, and the thermometer outside the living-room window, which often registered temperatures in the 80's, crept up to 105° in the sun. The beach, so appealing in September and October that it was used as a playground, gymnasium, and outdoor living room by young and old, became too hot for comfort as the December sun beat down, scorching the sand.

Most of the Americans retreated to the shady comfort of country-club pools, and Mr. Jamison joined Gavea in order to allow his family to escape from the apartment. Peggy started to take golf lessons after school in the afternoon, was told that she had a natural swing, and discovered that Carlos had been the runner-up in last year's intramural golf tournament.

"Would you be willing to play a round with me someday?" she proposed shyly. "I'm getting sort of tired of hitting bags of balls. But of course I'll be a frightful dub. . . . Maybe it would bore you to pieces."

Carlos was immediately gallant. "It wouldn't bore me at all. As a matter of fact," he admitted, with quick male assertiveness, "I might be able to give you some pointers. But let's put it off until school closes. Uncle João's been after me to pull up my grades on these exams, and I've promised to use all my spare time studying, the next two weeks."

The fortnight dragged for Peggy, but vacation loomed ahead, and to her parents' pleasure, she worked hard preparing for her own examinations. "I think Carlos is a good influence on the child," she overheard her mother remark to her father one evening. "I've never seen her so interested before."

The niggling feeling of guilt, which had continued to prick Peggy at intervals ever since the night of Guida's party, gave way to a realization that this was a very perceptive remark. She was interested not only in school; she was excited by everybody and everything around her. In fact, for the first time, she felt truly and abundantly alive!

How much of this expansive feeling was due to Carlos she didn't stop to analyze, but certainly Guida was almost as responsible as her brother for Peggy's increasing awareness of the complex quality of Rio. It was Guida who first took her to the Museum of Modern Art, Guida who introduced her to the botanical gardens where the Palma Mater—parent of every palm tree in Brazil—reached high into the sky. It was Guida, too, who had led her early one Saturday morning to a downtown *feira*, a noisy, bustling outdoor market, where everything from shoes to singing birds— from pigs' entrails to rare orchid plants—was for sale.

Booths crowded one another along the endless alleys, vendors hawked their wares in the accents of Amazonas or of São Paulo. Indians jostled Africans, Portuguese, and men of mixed bloods.

To Peggy the *feira* seemed as complicated and foreign as the serpentine mosaic sidewalk bordering Copacabana Beach. She hugged Guida's arm and wandered up and down the crowded aisles in fascination, sniffing the coffee, the herbs, the spices, and looking into faces of a thousand different shades. These people, she recognized, were more truly the Brazilians of the future than Guida and her aristocratic relatives. These were the people Carlos wanted to help!

Three days before Christmas, by prearrangement with Dona Plácida, Peggy paid her first visit to the *favela* clinic, where she was to work during the next two months. Her mother sent her off with considerable trepidation, not in the least mollified by the fact that the Almeidas were going with her.

"Wash your hands if you touch *anything!*" Mrs. Jamison cautioned. "Don't get too close to anybody's face. Now have you got plenty of Kleenex? I do really think they should provide you with nose masks." She started to wring her hands and murmured, "Oh dear, I don't really think this is a good idea."

"Face it, Mother, you can't keep me in cotton batting forever," Peggy said with a grin, but later, as she followed Dona Plácida and Guida up a winding, slippery mountain path, she became almost ill from the stench.

Tar-paper shanties clung to the mountain like insecure, bedraggled goats. Naked children, sometimes quite clean but more often filthy, stood back against the walls to stare curiously at the strangers invading their domain. Pariah dogs, skeleton-thin, scrabbled among piles of refuse. Radios blared, babies cried, and pregnant women, with buckets on their heads, waddled down the mountain toward a community hydrant.

Occasionally a man, lounging in a doorway, looked up at the trio sullenly, and once Peggy was accosted by an old crone, selling lottery tickets. "Just ignore her," Guida cautioned. "Come on!" At last they reached a low-lying, shedlike building painted gray and white, where a line, which had formed in front of the door, announced clearly, although wordlessly, that the doctor was within.

Dona Plácida took the girls around to a side entrance, leading into a *farmácia,* where a young nun in a white coif was pouring pills from a large bottle into a small one. She turned, greeting the Almeidas in Portuguese, then glanced at Peggy curiously.

"This is Margaret Jamison, a classmate of Guida's at the Escola Americana," explained Dona Plácida, still speaking Portuguese. "She is going to work with us here during vacation. Shall we start her off as we did Guida, with you?"

Peggy could catch only some of the words in the ensuing dialogue, because the two women spoke very rapidly, but within a few minutes it became clear that she was being turned over to the care of Sister Maria-Theresa for the remainder of the morning. Her mentor spoke only a few words of English, but by now Peggy had enough Portuguese, so that they could manage to communicate, and fortunately the labels on the bottles shelved along the sides of the crowded room were in the international language of medicine.

The sister started her new helper with an easy task, measuring thirty white pellets into a clearly marked prescription envelope. This operation Peggy repeated again and again, counting carefully as she sat on a high stool at a counter that faced a front window. Guida and her mother had disappeared, and from the general air of busyness about the clinic Peggy could surmise that she would see no more of them all morning. Sister Maria-Theresa came and went with prescription forms, beakers, and bottles. Every time the dispensary door opened into the crowded waiting room, Peggy could hear a murmur of voices and occasionally catch a glimpse of Dr. Vilaça opening his office door to admit the next patient, then closing it again quickly.

Carlos she did not see at all, and since no mention had been made of him on the way out, Peggy had no way of knowing whether he was here or not. It had been on the tip of her tongue to ask, "Where's Carlos?" but she hadn't wanted to seem prying or overanxious, so good manners held her back.

"Three, six, nine, twelve, fifteen, eighteen—" Peggy counted the pills automatically as the morning wore on. She had reduced the simple task to a factorylike formula, and was able to divide her attention between the white envelopes and the scene outside.

Shaded inadequately by ragged straw hats, parasols, or umbrellas, women and children stood patiently in line in the broiling sun. In the whole group there were only three men—a toothless, ancient Indian on a cane, a young blade in a neon-bright magenta shirt with his arm in a sling, and a middle-aged, surly-looking fellow with sores all over his face.

Peggy shuddered in disgust when she looked at him, and her mother's cautionary remarks became more understandable. How could Carlos and his uncle bear to treat such cases? They must have stomachs far stronger than hers. Putting aside still another sealed envelope of pills, she turned her attention to the children, forlorn little creatures with the protruding stomachs that signified malnutrition. "Banana bellies," they called them in Brazil.

She was so absorbed that she was not aware that someone other than the quiet-stepping nun had come into the dispensary, but suddenly Peggy found her eyes covered by hands that smelled of disinfectant. "Don't look if it distresses you so much," Carlos whispered into her ear.

Peggy pulled the hands away and turned her head with a welcoming smile, as her eyes discovered a new Carlos, workmanlike in a blue cotton jacket, which he tied down the back like a hospital gown. The narrow collar hugged his lean neck in Chinese style, and the faded color made his skin look ruddy and vital. He went over to another counter and picked up a bottle of iodine and some boxes of bandages. "I've got to hurry now, but I'll be back," he said.

Another dozen envelopes were filled before he returned. Then Peggy asked him a question which had been teasing her all morning. "What sort of diseases do these people have? Besides malnutrition, I mean."

Carlos gave a slight shrug. "Malaria and hookworm are probably the most common. But there's still lots of tuberculosis—and leprosy."

"Leprosy?" Peggy whispered the word in horror and glanced again at the man with the sores on his face. The skin on her arms rose in goose pimples. "I thought there were places for people like that."

"There are," replied Carlos calmly. "Leprosariums. Our government is establishing new ones all the time. And of course you know that now leprosy can be halted. A new specific has been discovered which does a remarkable job."

Sister Maria-Theresa, who had been busy over near the dispensary door, called to Carlos in Portuguese, and the boy said to Peggy, "It's time to distribute the milk ration. I think she could use your help."

Peggy was glad to climb down from her stool and stretch her legs, aware for the first time that another line of women and children had formed at the side. It was not bottled milk they awaited, but powdered milk, packaged in cartons, and as the two young women passed out the ration the haggard mothers murmured apathetic thanks, mumbling *obrigadas* which sounded more like "brigad."

The heat in the *farmácia* was by now well above 105°, and perspiration streamed down Peggy's face, dripping off the end of her nose. The whirring fan, attached to the center of the ceiling, did no more than disturb the air; it was almost as useless as the screen door, which admitted new platoons of flies every time it opened and shut.

Not a moment too soon, Dona Plácida and Guida appeared to tell Peggy the time had come to go home. The trio left the way they had arrived, and neither Carlos nor Dr. Vilaça put in an appearance to say good-by.

"They asked to be excused," Dona Plácida explained, with her quiet formality. "It has been a very trying morning. Two accident cases were brought in before we came—second-degree burns that had to be treated at once—and that held everything up."

Guida, unaware that such medical talk made revolting images swim before Peggy's eyes, and that her North American friend was getting dizzy from the heat and the *favela* odors, kept asking questions.

"Did you find it interesting? Isn't Sister Maria-Theresa nice? Did Carlos tell you that Uncle João has just received a medal for his research?"

Peggy answered automatically, trying not to stumble, trying not to breathe. How could Guida and her mother take this horrible slum, these scrofulous people, so much for granted? And how could they bear to come back here again and again?

The thought that she had committed herself to such

a routine for two mornings each week during the next two months made Peggy feel physically ill. When she climbed into the car, her lips grew white and her skin was cold and clammy with apprehension. Desperately sick at her stomach, she wasn't at all sure she could control herself until she reached home.

What she said during the ensuing conversation, how she took leave of the Almeidas, she scarcely knew. The ride up in the apartment elevator seemed to take a fortnight, and the route to the bathroom seemed longer than the yellow-brick road to the Land of Oz. When she emerged, fifteen minutes later, she was pale under her tan. Jacinta, concerned, met her in the kitchen door. "You feeling all right, *senhorita?*" she asked.

"I am now," Peggy answered, not quite truthfully, then countered with another question. "Is Mother home?"

When Jacinta shook her head Peggy was relieved. "I've been working at a *favela* clinic with Guida and Dona Plácida," she reminded the *baiana*. "Oh, Jacinta, how can people live that way? Like animals!"

A veil seemed to draw itself across Jacinta's limpid dark eyes. She put down a bowl she was drying and said, speaking with quiet sadness, "Most of the people who live there earn barely enough money to live at all. Less than one American dollar a day. And Rio is an expensive city. They have no choice."

"Then they shouldn't have so many children!" Peggy cried.

Jacinta smiled gently. "This is a Catholic country, *senhorita*. You forget."

"And radios!" persisted Peggy. "How can they buy radios if they can't buy food?"

Jacinta's smile became a chuckle. "Not all are so poor they have to live in the *favelas*," she admitted. "But some have become used to the shacks in which they live. Even if the government should build new apartments and invite them to move, they would resist. The *favela* is home."

Before Peggy could digest this astonishing information the hall door opened and her mother, laden with gaily wrapped packages, came laughing into the room. Behind her was Tobey, dragging a Casuarina tree taller than he by a good foot and a half.

"*Feliz Natal!*" he yelled.

Peggy got up from the chair arm where she had alighted and went toward him. "That's the most moth-eaten Christmas tree I've ever seen!"

"It isn't!" retorted Tobey, offended. "It's a gooder!"

Spilling her packages onto the sofa, Mrs. Jamison backed him up. "You should have seen the others. This one may be a little brown around the edges, but it's by far the best."

A trail of falling needles followed the course of the tree across the room to the corner where it would stand, and for the next two days the Jamisons were aware of a fairy patter of rain in the living room. By Christmas morning there were more needles on the floor than on the tree, and everyone had to dust them off the presents before opening them.

Peggy was rapturous over a gold bracelet with a topaz charm, given her by her parents. Tobey had a new surfboard, a beach ball, and several games. Mr. Jamison, at his special request, had received books, some about Brazil and others by Brazilian authors. To his wife, whom he jokingly claimed to be a woman of refinement but not of culture, because she read little except the daily papers, he had given a beautiful aquamarine dinner ring. Jacinta received an extra week's pay and some nylon stockings, which she regarded with awe. After all the presents had been opened, she collected and folded the wrapping paper and the ribbons as busily as a squirrel gathering nuts.

By ten o'clock the heat was so intense that it was hard to believe that in the United States there could be snow. Tobey and his father went down to see a sweating Santa Claus disembark from a helicopter at Santos Dumont Airport, but Peggy and her mother, still in cool negligees, lurked indoors until it was time to go out to Gavea Golf Club for a buffet lunch.

Here, as part of the North American celebration of the holiday, Santa, wearing a bright-red bathing suit, rode in to the beach on a surfboard, and the buffet table was laden with sliced cold turkey, ham, and every sort of accompanying delicacy.

Peggy helped herself frugally. Somehow the very quantity of food made her ill at ease. Up in the *favelas*, right now, how were they celebrating Christmas? She knew that the favorite present among the poor was a pair of shoes. But how many would receive even this humble gift?

It didn't help to remind herself that the Brazilians observed Christmas in quite a different manner from the North Americans. Here it remained a religious holiday. Presents were exchanged, but there was none of the extravagance, none of the commercialism, of Christmas in the United States.

She knew that in the Almeida home the day would be a quiet one. Last night, on Christmas Eve, Carlos and Guida had gone with their parents to midnight Mass, after which a dinner had been served to the family and a number of invited relatives.

Had Cleo been there? she wondered, with only the smallest twinge of envy. Somehow she no longer considered Carlos' "kissin' cousin" a threat.

Chapter 9

On New Year's Eve there were processions along the *avenidas,* and all night long lights flickered on the beach. Snatches of African music drifted into the apartment as a sporadic breeze lifted the curtains, and a certain restlessness hung in the air.

"What are the lights for?" Tobey asked curiously.

"There's a cult in Rio called *macumba,*" Mr. Jamison explained. "It's a combination of Catholicism and black magic, and this is the big night. There are all sorts of voodoo ceremonies all over town, with chickens offered as sacrifices. The candles are burned to propitiate the gods."

"You're kidding," Tobey accused his parent, but Peggy, whose experience in the *favela* was educating her in more ways than one, said, "No he's not."

Later that evening Tobey, impressed by his sister's new wisdom, came bounding into her bedroom. "Who believes all this *macumba* stuff?" he asked. "Jacinta?"

"I shouldn't think so," Peggy replied slowly. "But

you can't be sure. I wouldn't talk to her about it, if I were you. It's none of our business, anyway."

Tobey flopped down on the other twin bed and stared at the ceiling. "You sound like Mommy," he accused.

Peggy laughed, but she glanced over at her brother sharply. What else, she wondered, had their mother been unwilling to discuss? Inevitably, the feeling of guilt, which she had pushed back in her subconscious, leaped up and flickered for an instant like a candle flame. Then she returned to reading *Gone With the Wind,* which she had discovered in a downtown bookstore. It was a long and compelling novel, good for bedtime reading during vacation.

That night it was unusually hot and still in the apartment. Peggy slept fitfully, and was wide awake at dawn, uncomfortable in the rumpled bed. She got up, leaned on the window sill, then decided to slip into a bathing suit and go for a walk. This was not a particularly unusual thing to do, because Rio is an early-rising town. Already, although it was not yet six o'clock, a servant was walking a dog along the serpentine sidewalk and a barefoot old lady, dressed all in black, was hobbling across the sand.

Peggy watched her as she put down her cane at the tide line, took off the scarf that bound her gray hair, then waded into the water, fully clothed. When the waves reached her knees she dunked several times, scrubbed her face with her hands, then turned and squatted, so that the water could splash over her back.

After a while she came out of the sea, gathered up her belongings, and started back toward the mountains, dripping wet.

Peggy walked in the direction of Leblon, keeping to the cool sand along the water's edge and enjoying the sensation of being virtually alone beneath the arched sky. The washed beach at her feet bore no human footprints but hers, only the marks of shore birds, of the skittering of sandpipers, the webbed impressions of gulls. There was something mysterious and romantic about these tracks. They began nowhere, and vanished suddenly on the vast new floor left by the receding tide. In the early morning light the sand was the color of raw silk, rich and alive, a different substance from the dry corn meal above the tide line, pock-marked by yesterday's visitors.

Both sea and sand were so beautiful that Peggy began to think how wonderful it would be if, by some lucky chance, Carlos, too, had awakened early and decided to come for a walk on the beach. She deplored the Brazilian custom which did not permit the sort of dating she was accustomed to at home. Ever since school closed she had seen Carlos only twice—when they had played around the golf course at Gavea —except for the mornings at the clinic. And this was not enough, not nearly enough! She'd have to arrange a swimming party at the club, a trip to the zoo, or something involving a crowd, so that they could be together again soon.

The orange sun floated higher and higher into the

sky while Peggy walked on, plotting dreamily, the sound of the ocean in her ears. Great waves rolled in from the Atlantic, following each other, to fling themselves down, fulfilled and destroyed within a moment's space.

Along the *avenida* cars and buses began to scamper toward the city, but Peggy was scarcely aware of them, because the noise of their motors was drowned in the boom and watery tumbling of the surf. She walked as far as the street that led back to the Almeida's house, then stopped and stood staring inland, as though she had reached her destination, as though her delight in the morning was empty now that it was time to turn and go home.

It was here that Tobey caught up with her, running up, wide-eyed, to announce, "There's a dead chicken in a hole up there, just the way Daddy said. I thought dead chickens were to eat."

Peggy didn't reply. "How did you get out here?" she asked instead.

"I saw you from the window," said Tobey innocently. "Why? Don't you want me?" He sounded hurt.

And because he looked so skinny and small and suddenly baffled, a surge of affection swept Peggy, a sisterly feeling that always asserted itself without warning at odd and unexpected times. "I just wondered," she said, grinning down at the boy. "I was just surprised to see you, that's all."

Tobey grinned back, reassured and companionable now. "Been swimming yet?" he asked.

Peggy shook her head. "The flags aren't up. It's not allowed."

Out of sheer exuberance, Tobey ran around his sister in a circle, then stopped and asked, pointing away from the sea, "Isn't that the street where Carlos lives?"

Peggy, startled, nodded as though she hadn't been aware of it. "Yes, I guess it is."

"You like Carlos, don't you? He's your friend."

"Yes," Peggy admitted. "Guida is my friend too."

"But Carlos especially," Tobey said with perspicacity. "Just like Ernie is my friend. We go places together. We talk."

He really is an endearing child sometimes, Peggy thought, as she smiled down at her brother, remembering the time when, at the age of four, he had brought home an imaginary playmate called Littlechick. Littlechick had lived with the family for the entire week end, with a place set at the table and a special pillow added to Tobey's bed.

"Do you remember Littlechick?" Peggy asked now.

Tobey frowned. "Ernie is my *real* friend," he replied.

"Do I know Ernie?" Peggy had trouble sorting out Tobey's playmates. "Is he one of the boys you meet on the beach?"

"Sometimes," said Tobey. "He's in my class at school and his father is a taxi driver and his mother works at Mesbla." He added, rather proudly, "Ernie is an only child."

This was indeed unusual in Rio, where big families were the rule. Twenty children living under one roof were not uncommon, and Peggy had heard stories of sixty offspring being born to a single father who had been married three times. But this was scarcely conversational material for a chat with Tobey. "Where does Ernie live?" she asked.

"Back near the school," said Tobey promptly. "His real name's Ernesto, of course. Sometimes I walk home with him afternoons. He has a parrot who can say, 'Não importa' very plainly. You ought to hear!"

"I'd like to. Is the parrot tame?"

"Not very. He lets Ernie pat him, but he'd bite me."

This announcement was almost lost in the crash of a foaming comber, its heavy overspill followed by a loud withdrawing roar. Tobey glanced at the ocean. "Maybe by the time we get back to our place the flag will be up," he suggested hopefully.

During the next few days Peggy completely forgot about Ernesto. She and Becky promoted a trip to the zoo, set for the first cool day, but meanwhile she went twice to the clinic with the Almeidas, and each time it became a little easier and more interesting. She was rewarded by a look of approval, which was almost affection, in Dona Plácida's eyes, and by the outspoken compliments of both Guida and Carlos, who confessed that they weren't at all sure—after that first visit—that she'd ever come back.

Peggy laughed and chided them for their lack of confidence, unwilling to admit that each trip to the *favela* took courage of a sort. "I'm just not the Florence Nightingale type," she confessed to Becky one hot afternoon, as the two girls lay on towels beside the Gavea pool. "But if Guida can take it, I guess I can. And as for Carlos—he's really in his element."

Mrs. Jamison was playing bridge with some acquaintances in the shade of the clubhouse balcony, and later on she came down to collect Peggy and take her home. No sooner had they arrived at the apartment than Tobey burst in, bearing a battered suitcase. His eyes were shining, and with his free hand he was dragging a shy, slender child of his own age, with skin the color of milk chocolate and the limpid, wild eyes of a fawn.

"This is Ernie," he announced proudly. "His mother has been taken to the hospital for some tests, so I've invited him to spend the night."

Mrs. Jamison's gasp was quickly stifled. "Hello, Ernie," she said, in a tone that was curiously flat. Peggy glanced from her mother to Tobey, and then to his great and good friend Ernesto, who looked as frightened as a puppy snatched from the nest. "Hello, Ernie," she repeated, anxious to sound more welcoming.

"Boa tarde, senhora, senhorita." Ernesto's voice was pitched just above a whisper, as his eyes moved from Tobey's mother to his sister, and back to the mother again. It was obvious that he spoke no English, but Tobey's Portuguese was equal to the occasion. "Come with me," he invited. "Come to my room—*meu quarto.*"

"Com licença," murmured Ernesto, as he edged past Peggy. Ill at ease though he was, he spoke with the

good manners she had come to expect of Brazilians, and then fled in Tobey's wake.

Immediately Mrs. Jamison turned to her daughter. "I knew the whole thing was a mistake from the start."

Peggy pretended not to understand. "What was a mistake, Mother?"

"Why, playing with those boys on the beach. I told you he might bring one of them to the house, and now he has."

Annoyance flared in Peggy like a torch, but she tried to hide it. "Ernesto is Tobey's best friend," she tried to explain.

"I know. That's just it. A nigra! The child simply doesn't understand." Mrs. Jamison nervously twisted the aquamarine ring on her right hand. "Now what are we going to do?"

In a cool and level voice that concealed her inner upheaval, Peggy suggested, "I guess we'd better tell Jacinta to lay another place at the table. You certainly aren't thinking of turning the boy out?"

Yet, a second later, when her mother avoided meeting her eyes, Peggy knew that this was just what she had been considering. Shame conquered the impulse, and Mrs. Jamison bowed to an immediate fate, but there was no doubt that the situation was strained. Fortunately, Mr. Jamison, upon being introduced to Tobey's young guest when he arrived home from the office, seemed to find Ernie perfectly acceptable, and treated the child quite normally. But Peggy over-did her effort to be kind, and her mother retreated into a shell as complex as that of a nautilus. She was, Peggy realized, completely unequal to a situation where she was required to relax her standards, which were as inflexible as the morals of the Southern gentlewoman by whom she had been raised.

Tobey, aglow with possessiveness and delight at having a house guest, was not yet aware of any tension, but Peggy reacted to her mother's feelings as to an electric shock. Sitting at the dinner table opposite the two boys, she felt as though she didn't belong to this family. It was like living through a nightmare, and although the conversation was deliberately superficial, she felt as though the meal would never end.

Yet, although Peggy's sympathies were with Tobey and with this frightened child who had been offered a haven here while his mother was away, she had never felt more compassion for her mother, who couldn't help her background any more than she could escape it. Segregation had hardened around her life like cement.

Peggy suffered not only for her mother, but for herself, because her own guilt feelings were newly ready to leap to the surface whenever the color question was challenged. Was *she* so much better, hiding her secret about Carlos, assuming an intellectual tolerance that was a spiritual fraud?

Who is going to stop all this color thing? she wondered. Is it going to go on and on and on? But how can I do anything? Custom is against me; my own mother is against me. And in a way she's right. Back home we couldn't have Ernesto to dinner. She knows, and I know—even though Tobey doesn't realize—that someday we'll be going back.

Peggy felt as though she were standing on a bridge between the generations, a suspension bridge such as llamas were always seen crossing in pictures about Peru. Tobey was on one side, innocent and unsuspecting, and her mother on the other, too indoctrinated, too aware. Her father, bless his heart, was reaching out a hand to help her, although he didn't really understand why his daughter was so scared.

"Jacinta, will you bring the boys more milk with dessert?" The familiar voice almost—almost!—sprung the trap which seemed to be blocking Peggy's path.

Milk . . . dessert . . . bedtime. She got a firm grip on reality, but late that night she could hear voices from her parents' bedroom, and while she could distinguish no words Peggy knew that they were arguing a question for which there was no answer in their generation, and perhaps not even in hers.

But in Tobey's—? Peggy lay, tight-chested, in the dark. Maybe for Tobey there was an answer. Even an answer like Ernesto—a dear and good friend.

Chapter 10

The baby was encrusted with filth, wrapped in clay
of its own ordure. "Here, take it," Sister Maria-Theresa
said to Peggy, as she carried the reeking bundle into
the *farmácia*. "Run some warm water into a basin and
see if you can clean it up."

Peggy gagged, but there was no time for refusal.
The Sister had turned on her rubber heel and was
out the door again before she could frame a reply.

Alone with the task before her, Peggy laid the infant, which seemed subhuman even in its grunting
wail, on a counter top, and ran the water, testing its
temperature with her elbow as she had been taught.
Retching with distaste, she put the creature into the
bath, supporting the pear-shaped head with one hand
while she let some of the dirt soak off.

Eventually the shape of the infant became apparent.
Peggy changed the water, found a cotton sponge, and
realized that she was bathing a baby girl. The little
thing, lulled by the warmth, stopped crying, but it was

so weak that Peggy became afraid it would die in the bath.

What manner of mother can this child have? Peggy wondered, as disgust fought with pity. Even an animal licks its young clean. With her free hand she twisted a bit of absorbent cotton on a stick, dipped it in a bottle of oil, and poked tentatively at the tiny ears. She wished somebody would come tell her what to do next.

But the door remained stubbornly closed, as sounds from the waiting room testified to a busy post-holiday morning. At the *macumba* celebrations there had doubtless been all sorts of accidents, and the doctor and his staff were overwhelmed.

When the baby was as clean as Peggy could manage to get it, she dried the raw, irritated skin with a soft towel and poured oil over the entire body, smoothing it gently with her fingers, then wrapped it up like a mummy, with only the head showing, and laid it in an empty cardboard carton.

"I suppose I ought to feed you," she said aloud. "But what?" Formulas and sterilized bottles flashed into her mind, things she knew nothing about.

A moment later Sister Maria-Theresa came through the door, followed by a dull-eyed girl in her early teens, who was wearing a ragged blue skirt and a dirty sleeveless blouse, which clung to her upstanding breasts. At the Sister's command, she stripped off the shirt and stood naked from the waist up, then took the soap she was handed and started to wash at the sink. A tentative smile broke over her face, as though she found this pure nonsense. The baby was crying again, but she completely ignored it until the Sister handed it to her to nurse.

Then she unwrapped the bundle and looked at the infant in dazed surprise, followed by a rapid stream of protest. Peggy could catch only an occasional word, but she gathered that she was accusing the Sister of substituting another child.

Sister Maria-Theresa was patient. "This is your baby, but now it is clean," she said. "This *senhorita americana* has washed it, just as you must wash it from now on, every day."

She showed the *favelada* how to fill the basin, how to test the water, how to swab the eyes and the ears, and gradually a gleam of interest replaced the dullness in the girl's eyes. After the baby finished nursing, the Sister explained how to fold and pin a diaper, and gave the mother a package of cotton squares to take along home. With every sentence the nun stressed the importance of cleanliness, then went on to tell the girl about the danger of disease in the *favela,* and extracted a promise that she would return to the clinic the next week.

When the patients had left, Sister Maria-Theresa turned to Peggy with sad eyes. "By next week," she admitted, sighing, "the baby may be dead."

Before Peggy could reply Carlos burst into the *farmácia.* Looking anxious and concerned, he asked quickly, "What did you do with that horrible infant that came in this morning? My uncle says it's the worst case of neglect he's ever seen."

"The *senhorita* managed to clean her up," said Sister Maria-Theresa, then turned to Peggy. "It isn't that the mother is cruel, you know," she said, in slow, understandable Portuguese. "She is only a child herself, and she doesn't know any better, that's all."

Carlos wasn't listening to the nun. He was staring at Peggy. "*You?*"

Peggy didn't know what to make of such incredulity. "There was nobody else here," she tried to explain.

"I couldn't have touched it," Carlos was saying with a shudder. "I don't see how—" Then his eyes filled with sudden respect, and he came over and took Peggy's shoulders and kissed her on both cheeks. "You are a truly wonderful girl," he told her in English, while the nun stood by and smiled appreciatively.

The warmth of Carlos' approval was matched by his mother and sister, and from that day on Peggy was no longer an outsider. She was a member of a team. Dona Plácida treated her with growing cordiality, Dr. Vilaça patted her shoulder whenever he came near enough, and Guida treated her as a confidante as well as a special friend.

Meanwhile the heat increased, rather than abated. By mid-January even a brisk night breeze was unequal to the task of cooling the air in the apartment, and the overhead fans worked ceaselessly but in vain. Mrs. Jamison talked of searching for some place with air-conditioning, but the weather made her listless, and she spent most of her time at Gavea, fanning herself on the edge of the pool.

Tobey no longer went to the beach, except in the very early morning. The sand was too burning-hot, even for him. One noon, returning from the clinic, Peggy found her brother wandering around the apartment disconsolately.

"Haven't you got anything to do?" she asked, when he followed her into her bedroom. "What's happened to all your pals?"

Tobey didn't answer. He sat on a chair and swung his scratched and bitten legs to and fro, frowning at his toes. "Why doesn't Mommy like Ernesto?" he asked after a while.

"Doesn't she?" Peggy hedged, because she was startled that Tobey was so certain.

Tobey shook his head. "She says he's—he's undesirable. What does that mean?"

Peggy bit her lip. How could she reply?

"Does it mean he's colored?" Tobey asked, swinging his legs a little faster.

"No," Peggy replied unhappily. "It doesn't mean that."

Tobey let out his breath in a whoosh, looking relieved. "Well, that's good," he said, and suddenly slipped down from the chair and raced out to the living room.

But Peggy stood where he had left her, and felt her eyelids sting with tears. She knew that she should go out and find Tobey and try to tell him the truth but she couldn't face it. Maybe later, but not now, not right this minute. She simply wasn't that brave.

At lunch, for which Mrs. Jamison was out, Peggy tried to make amends for her lack of courage. She offered to play parcheesi with Tobey, although it was a game she found infinitely boring, and for an hour she stifled her yawns as she repeatedly rattled a pair of dice in a cardboard cup.

When Becky called, about three o'clock, to say a crowd from school was going to an air-cooled movie, and didn't she want to come along, Peggy escaped gratefully. She had seen the film before, but it was the lesser of two evils, and she joined the group in the theater lobby, feeling as though she had been reprieved from jail.

To her immediate delight, she discovered that Carlos was along, and he managed to arrange things so that they sat beside each other in the dark. Almost at once he reached for her hand and slipped it under his arm, squeezing the fingers companionably.

Companionably—and something more! Something that made a tingle of pleasure creep up Peggy's spine. She smiled at Carlos and he smiled back, his black eyes teasing.

"I've missed you," he whispered.

"You just saw me this morning!" Peggy reminded him with a chuckle.

"The clinic doesn't count."

Peggy couldn't contradict this statement. She sat quiet and tried to concentrate on the newsreel, but she was thrillingly aware of the pressure of Carlos' hand.

"Where's Guida?" she whispered after a while, more from nervousness than from curiosity.

"Gone shopping with *Mamãe*," Carlos answered promptly. "We're getting ready to go on vacation, you know."

Peggy hadn't known. Shocked, she tried to pull her hand away, but Carlos tightened his grip. "When are you going?" Peggy asked, feeling her voice grow squeaky with dismay.

"To our summer place," Carlos answered, misunderstanding.

"I said, 'When?'"

"Oh, not for a couple of weeks. We always go to the mountains the first of February, you see."

"But what about the clinic?" queried Peggy, while on her other side Becky said, "Sh!" in mild annoyance.

Carlos shrugged. "Uncle João always manages to fill in somehow with other volunteers."

"Sh!" cautioned Becky again, more definitely, and Peggy subsided, but although she kept her eyes on the screen she paid no attention to the flickering images there. She felt more lonely than Tobey had looked at noon.

The next time she went to the clinic with the Almeidas she was unusually quiet. Although she knew it was unreasonable, she felt that she had been cheated, that Dona Plácida should have explained, right at the beginning, about the family vacation. It was another hot, humid day, and she stood for two hours measur-

ing out medicines in the *farmácia,* and then, quite unexpectedly, as she was crossing the room with a beaker
of alcohol, everything began to spin and grow black
before her eyes, and she slipped quietly to the floor.

It was Dr. Vilaça, coming into the dispensary with
a request for some extra supplies for the office, who
found her. Peggy awakened to find her clothes soaked
with alcohol and to the feeling that something peculiar
had happened quite a long time ago.

"Wh-what did I do?" she stammered, trying to sit
up.

"Lie right where you are," the doctor ordered. "You
must have fainted. I'll send my sister in to you at once."

Dona Plácida's eyes were full of concern. "It's the
heat," she decided. "You've been working too hard,
and you're not accustomed to our climate. I blame
myself."

"Oh, no," Peggy tried to protest, but she felt weak
and uncertain. She closed her eyes again and tried to
pull herself together, but it was several minutes before
she could manage to raise her head.

By now Carlos and Guida had also appeared on the
scene, and between them they got Peggy to a chair
and ordered her to stay there until it was time to leave.
On the way down the hill she felt tottery and uncertain, but with the young Almeidas on either side she
managed to get to the car.

That evening Dona Plácida sent a note around to
the apartment. It was addressed to Mrs. Jamison, and
it contained a thoroughly unexpected invitation for

Peggy. The Almeidas would be delighted if she could spend a week with them at their summer home in Petrópolis.

Peggy, quite recovered from her morning's collapse, could scarcely believe her eyes. She read the note again and again, anticipation mounting, until she was in a positive fever of excitement.

Her mother, however, was not quite as enthusiastic. "I don't know that I want you going off to stay with a family I've never even met."

"You know Guida and Carlos," Peggy reminded her. "You like them, don't you? You think they're all right."

"I just feel that Mrs. Almeida—*Senhora*, I mean—should call on me. If the situation were reversed, I can assure you—"

"But the situation isn't reversed," Peggy broke in. She came over and knelt in supplication by her mother's chair. "Please, Mother, please don't be stuffy and stand on formalities. Please say I can go!"

Finally Mrs. Jamison was persuaded, on the basis that Peggy would actually be Guida's guest, and that she knew Guida well by now and liked her very much. Mr. Jamison spread out a road map on the dining-room table and located Petrópolis, which sounded to Peggy rather like a Greek amphitheater, but which turned out to be a resort in the mountains about two hours' drive from the Avenida Atlântica.

There followed, inevitably, a good deal of fuss about arrangements, but it was finally decided that Peggy should be driven to the mountains by her family on the first Saturday in February, and this suited everyone.

"Now I'll be able to meet your Dona Plácida," said Mrs. Jamison happily to her daughter. "It will make me feel much easier about leaving you in her care."

"I never knew anybody so old-fashioned!" Peggy complained, half-teasing, half-serious. Infiltrating her natural anticipation, however, was a seeping fear. Suppose Guida's grandmother was there?

This, of course, was more than possible; it was very likely. These Brazilian families lived and traveled in great groups, and it was perfectly probable that the Petrópolis place might be the grandmother's own house.

At this point the fire of guilt, which Peggy had dampened for so long, flamed up anew. She tried to find words in which to explain the whole thing to her mother, and even rehearsed a speech aloud, before her mirror, sounding infinitely blasé and superior. But there was never a proper time, never a moment when she could launch a subject so risky. Besides, what could she possibly gain? At best, a Southerner's reluctant, disapproving acceptance of an unthinkable situation; at worst, a decision that Peggy would have to manufacture a last-minute excuse and stay home.

So she still kept her secret, treading softly through the days, nervous as a cat and torn between loyalty to her family and eagerness to be with Carlos.

A whole week in the same house! Her heart sang.

But suppose the grandmother is there? Can I be sure Mother won't create a scene?

It was conceivable that Peggy might have confided in her father, but on the one opportunity when she managed to get him alone, Tobey interrupted with a broken kite to be mended, and the moment was lost.

On the surface Peggy was just normally excited by her approaching trip. She mended shoulder straps on her slips, sewed on a button which had been lost from her best pajamas, pressed half a dozen cotton dresses and folded them, with tissue paper, into her suitcase, and helped her mother select a house present for her hostess, but all the time she felt as though she were living on a volcano which might suddenly erupt.

And then a fortuitous thing happened. Mrs. Jamison caught a really bad summer cold, ran a temperature, and was sent to bed by the doctor on the night before Peggy was due to arrive in Petrópolis.

"You go along with Dad and Tobey, dear," she said the next morning, between sneezes. "Jacinta will take good care of me."

Jacinta smiled from the doorway, confirming this prediction with a nod. "Plenty of liquids, that's the answer. I'll get some ripe *abacaxí* and squeeze the juice."

Mr. Jamison blew his wife a kiss from across the room. "I'll hurry right home! Now don't on any account get out of bed."

" 'By, darling. Please don't worry. Have a marvelous time, Peggy dear!"

Her mother looked so pretty and pathetic, propped up on pillows in the big bed, that Peggy instinctively drew closer to say good-by, but Mrs. Jamison put a hand up to ward her off. "Germs, sweetie. You don't want to catch my cold."

Beaming as though she enjoyed nothing more than responsibility, Jacinta saw them off at the door. "*Adeus, senhorita,*" she said, breaking into Portuguese in her excitement. Then she hugged Tobey, as though he were leaving on a long trip, and calling, "*Êle é nosso!*" waved good-by.

Relief at a possible crisis averted made Peggy beam with good humor as the little car rolled down the boulevard and joined a stream of other vehicles bound for the mountains. By now Mr. Jamison was as accustomed to Rio traffic as though he had lived here all his life. The highway to Petrópolis branched off out near the International Airport, and led toward green hills, wrapped with mist. As the hour advanced the sky cleared, and the hills became mountains, up which a white ribbon of a road curved over bridges and through tunnels, until it was lost in a concealing ridge.

"This is the Organ Range," Mr. Jamison told his children. "*Serra dos Órgãos.* There's a lookout spot about halfway up where we can stop."

But long before this Tobey begged to buy a bunch of the little finger bananas being hawked by roadside vendors. Then Mr. Jamison pulled up at the side of the road to get out his camera and take a picture of two amusing small boys and their donkey. "If we get there by noon we'll be lucky!" teased Peggy, laughing. "Poor Mother! Expecting you home before lunch."

Actually, all three of them were in a holiday mood. As the car climbed, the air cooled, and by the time they reached the outskirts of Petrópolis they felt as though they had entered a different world.

It was a garden city. Red, magenta, pink, and white impatiens blossoms covered the cliffs that bordered the road. Royal poinciana trees waved their great scarlet flowers overhead; yellow acacia spread its feathery blooms; bougainvillaea, hibiscus, and hydrangeas competed with color. Orchids dripped from overhead branches, and yellow lilies grew wild along the roadside. Amid this profusion silver trees turned over their green leaves, washed a metallic gray by the sun.

"It looks like something dreamed up by Disney," commented Peggy, and Tobey, in an automatic reflex, started to hum the song of the seven dwarfs.

Countering, Mr. Jamison burst forth with "O what a beautiful morning!" and thus the trio arrived in the center of town.

Directions were asked and given—on the one hand, in careful Portuguese; on the other, with grins and a spontaneous flow of unintelligible words and barely intelligible gestures. Yet within five minutes the Jamisons found themselves at the Almeida house, a square, dove-gray dwelling, eyelashed by decorative wrought-

iron balconies and set well back on a green lawn behind a Victorian spiked fence. It faced a canal, which
led to the approach of a baroque church, and it immediately seemed to Peggy the most enchanting house
she had ever seen.

Chapter 11

On her first morning in Petrópolis Peggy awakened to
the sound of the *sabiá*. The Brazilian nightingale was
singing from a thicket within an ancient bougainvillaea
which dripped purple blossoms on the balcony outside
the room where she and Guida slept.

The house was not yet stirring, and Peggy was glad,
because she wanted to relive yesterday, to go back over
the time and press it into her memory, as one would
preserve a flower between the pages of a book.

Dona Plácida, with Guida and Carlos, had been in
the hall to welcome her. After Mr. Jamison and Tobey
had been introduced and offered the *cafèzinhos* with
which every arrival is celebrated, they had given Peggy
over to the Almeidas' keeping and left to make up for
lost time on their return trip to Rio.

Now Peggy walked alone into a new world, following Guida up the curving stairs to a big square bedroom and soaking up impressions like a sponge.

Carlos, looking up at her from the tiled floor below
and winking solemnly, as though they shared a secret.

Big square rooms, with high ceilings, frescoed in fanciful scenes so old and faded that they were like pictures painted under water. Lunch, served in a vine-covered patio, opening on a garden full of flowers and tropical fruit trees. Carlos, attentive and smiling, pulling out his mother's chair, then coming around to sit beside his sister's guest.

For Peggy was *Guida's* guest. Dona Plácida's attitude left no question of that, and somehow it lent a certain piquancy to her relationship with Carlos. The sense of sharing a secret grew as the day advanced, and the excitement of being in the same house with a boy for whom she had such a very special feeling made Peggy feel as though she were living in a dream.

Siesta—the inevitable siesta. Shutters half-closed, light filtering through to glint on the polished bedroom floor, the carved baroque chest, and on Guida's tumbled hair. The squawk of a macaw from the garden, the flash of a blue-green parakeet.

Carlos again, reading in the patio, getting to his feet with quick courtesy when the girls appeared. The expression of approval as his eyes swept Peggy. Was it the yellow linen dress? From now on I'll love that dress, Peggy thought, as she lay listening to the *sabiá*, singing all the songs that rightfully should have been saved for night.

Raising herself on one elbow, Peggy glanced over at Guida, curled up like a kitten beneath the white sheet still sound asleep. She lay back and allowed herself to drift back in time once more, still savoring yesterday.

Senhor Alfredo's arrival from Rio, with Carlos hurrying to take his father's bag and Guida running to hug the autocratic, mustached gentleman Peggy remembered only dimly from the night of the birthday party. *Cafèzinho* again, with the sun dropping behind the church at the end of the canal. Uniformed maids carrying the *senhor's* luggage. The tinkling of a distant bell, and Carlos saying, "That must be grandmother. She has an intuition, Papa, that tells her you have arrived."

Closing her eyes, Peggy could see the scene that followed as clearly as though it were etched. Carlos, running up the stairs two at a time, then coming back down very slowly, step after careful step, with the old, white-haired lady clinging to his arm.

No longer needing to fear this encounter, Peggy found herself curious. So fragile and wrinkled that she looked scarcely real, Dona Virgilia had eyes as bright as buttons. Although she spoke little English her mind was keen, and she greeted the North American girl as though she could place her precisely.

Now Peggy's impressions melted again from the particular into a medley of sights and sounds. The enveloping warmth of the Brazilian family, one for the other. Guida running for a footstool, Senhor Alfredo presenting a box of candy, Dona Virgilia's surprisingly resonant voice. Dinner at a big table in the cool, dim dining room. The wonderful odor of curious Brazilian dishes, and the marvelous taste of chicken legs, wrapped in a creamy paste, breaded, and fried. *Coxinhas,* the Almeidas called them. She must try to remember the name.

Peggy stretched and smiled, coming now to the best part of the day, the evening, when there had been a band concert in the park. With Carlos as escort, the girls strolled along the tree-lined streets toward the sound of music, and Peggy found herself suddenly caught up in a scene straight out of the past.

The park, green in the lamplight, black in the shadows, and in the center the bandstand, glittering like a diamond on a velvet cloth. Paths alive with young people, groups of carefully dressed girls walking together, and—always going in the opposite direction—groups of boys.

"But why? What are they all doing?" Peggy had asked.

"This is the *passeio,*" Carlos explained. "It is a custom as old as Brazil. Guida will take you strolling. You will see."

"Can't you come too?"

Carlos shook his head, and he and his sister both laughed, but he looked flattered by Peggy's disappointment. "I couldn't be sorrier!"

"We'll meet him again in half an hour," Guida promised, appearing eager to be off. Peggy detected a nervousness in her manner that was surprising. She started off beside her friend, feeling completely at sea.

Quickly, however, she realized that she was herself part of a romantic ceremony, to which there was a definite routine. The boys and girls, walking by two's and three's, passed each other twice in one complete turn around the park. At first Guida appeared to be paying little attention to the young men who passed, but suddenly she caught her breath and whispered to Peggy, "There he is. See! The one on the left."

"Who?"

"Raymundo." Guida's voice was as soft as the clouds drifting in the starry sky, and her eyelashes fluttered becomingly. "His family lives near ours in Rio, and he has been coming here summers for ages and ages, but last night he smiled at me!"

Peggy was caught between amusement and wonder. This wasn't the Guida she knew, this trembling girl. The emancipation of the Escola Americana no longer surrounding her, she had become almost quaintly Brazilian, accepting the *passeio* as a serious courting dance. It was sweet, in a way, and touching, but it also seemed to belong to another age.

Carlos passed, walking alone, whistling. He turned to stare after Peggy, boldly, and she was conscious that he was again teasing. But Guida cautioned, "Don't turn your head." Peggy suppressed a giggle, and then walked along rather stiffly, aware that her fair skin and red hair were attracting attention, and that a dozen boys were trying to catch her eye. Then Raymundo passed again, and smiled openly at Guida, who blushed furiously. "Don't you think he's attractive?" she asked, after he had gone by.

"Not half so attractive as Carlos," Peggy wanted to

say, but she stifled the impulse and nodded, then turned her attention to a guitarist, who was strumming a popular love song in competition with the band. From the mountains came a breeze which stirred the slender palm trees and carried around the park a scent of jasmine and roses. It was all incredibly romantic, but Peggy hoped the half hour would soon be up.

Walking back home, Carlos, with unabashed intimacy, had taken her arm. Guida, drifting in her private dream, scarcely noticed, but Peggy was piercingly aware of the touch of his fingers. This was the moment in the evening at which her mind stopped and began to circle. Carlos, laughing down at her. Carlos, on a sudden impulse, turning to sweep her into his arms and dance a few steps to the distant band music. Carlos, leading the way into the empty kitchen to forage for something to eat.

Lying in bed this morning, Peggy could still smell the fragrant herbs hung in bunches near the kitchen chimney. She could see the clay-and-tile stove with its great iron oven, and the picture of St. Benedict hung on the wall to guarantee a plentiful supply of food to this house. In the refrigerator there was cold milk, goiabada—a guava paste—and fresh goat's cheese. Peggy wasn't hungry, but with a pleasure that amounted to love, she sat at the scrubbed kitchen table watching Carlos and Guida eat. She felt warmed by their friendship, and loved in return, as though this Brazilian family had flung its doors wide to take her in.

Guida stirred in the next bed, turning over on her

back to stretch and yawn. She turned her head toward Peggy and opened her eyes. "Hi," she said, using the Americanism naturally. "How long have you been awake?"

"Not long," Peggy fibbed. She swung her feet to the floor and hurried over to open the shutters. The air, still dewy fresh, was mountain-cool. "It's a perfectly divine morning!"

Guida chuckled at the use of the word "divine." "Very appropriate, since it's Sunday." She added, "There's a Protestant church on the other side of the square. Or would you like to come with us to Mass?"

Peggy had never been to Mass, but it seemed the thing to do to join the Almeida family. Senhor Alfredo drove his wife and Dona Virgilia in the car, but the young people walked, and on the way Peggy was introduced to still another facet of Carlos' personality.

He was sober this morning, dignified, accompanying the girls quietly and genuflecting with decorum as he entered the gilded and candlelit church. The Latin chants, the murmured responses, even the music, was strange to Peggy, used to a plain Presbyterian service. She stood, feeling constrained, while the others knelt and stood and knelt again, in obedience to signals only the initiated could understand. Could it be that Carlos was devout? The implications of Catholicism had never concerned Peggy. She had accepted Brazil as a Roman Catholic country, the Almeidas as a Roman Catholic family, but the baroque churches had looked like pretty wedding cakes, and the faith of the people who went there to worship had seemed as remote as the painted Virgins, glass-encased and unreal.

Peggy became vaguely troubled, and was glad when the priest and his acolytes retreated into the vestry and she could get out into the sunlight, where the Almeidas behaved understandably once more.

The square gray house, set on its carpet of green lawn, looked especially welcoming. Dr. João, up from Rio for Sunday lunch, was waiting on the terrace, the emerald ring of his profession flashing in the noonday light, and he had a surprise for them sitting in a wicker chair under the vine—a surprise with long, elegant legs and shining black hair—Cleo Andrade.

"I brought Cleo along to stay for a few days," Dr. João announced, with the easy confidence of a member of the family. "The heat is really quite unbearable, and she's looking exhausted, poor child."

To Peggy, Cleo didn't appear exhausted at all; she looked positively radiant, and turned her smile on everyone, but especially on Carlos. "I hope you're glad to see me," she said.

"I'm always glad to see you," Carlos replied, with quick courtesy, while Peggy stiffened, slightly and Guida said happily, "The more the merrier!"

If Peggy didn't share this sentiment she tried to conceal it, reminding herself that Cleo was a cousin in this family and that it was she who was the stranger in the house. It was perfectly natural that Cleo should be seated on Senhor Alfredo's right at lunch and helped first, after the hostess, to *feijoada*. Since Peggy was sharing Guida's room it was quite understandable that Cleo should be given the big guest chamber containing the bed that had once belonged to the royal family, when Petrópolis had been the Emperor's summer residence.

Apparently the Almeidas enjoyed pampering their new visitor, and Cleo accepted their attentions gracefully. She was charming to Dona Plácida and Dona Virgilia, to Guida and even to Peggy, whom she seemed to accept—as did the rest of the household—as Guida's guest.

To Carlos, Cleo's coming seemed to pose a problem. He wasn't rude to her, but he was indifferent, and Peggy could tell that he was almost as disappointed as she.

It raised her spirits a bit when he came right out with his chagrin, during a stolen moment on the upper curve of the stairs, where a *monstera deliciosa* spread green, concealing leaves. "Confound the luck," he whispered. "Why did she have to come, when I was counting on a week alone with you?"

"Well, not quite alone," Peggy reminded him lightly, although her heartbeat quickened.

Carlos grinned. "Never mind, we'll fix something. Can you ride a bicycle?"

Chapter 12

The next morning, by a sleight of hand Peggy didn't quite understand, but accepted joyfully, she found herself bicycling with Carlos to visit an orchid farm high in the hills. Diplomatically, but nonetheless firmly, Cleo had been persuaded that it would be very unwise to attempt such a trip, and Guida had offered to stay at home and keep her cousin company.

Carlos was in high spirits, pleased with his cleverness in getting Peggy off alone. She suspected that his mother had hesitated over allowing them such liberty, but had relented on the score that as a North American Peggy wasn't subject to the same restrictions as a Brazilian girl.

It didn't matter, anyway. It was enough that they were together, here in the country with its lush, fertile earth, its mango and papaya trees, its fragrant flowers. There was a fountain of spring water, a relic of colonial times, built into a wall, and they stopped and drank, then moved into the shade of a roadside tree and sat on the grass.

"Tired?" Carlos asked.

"Not at all." She smiled, plucked a long blade of grass, and nibbled at it. "Carlos—"

"Yes?"

"If we're back in the United States when you come to college, will you visit us in North Carolina?"

"I'd certainly try!" Carlos replied, but his eyes clouded for a moment. "Let's not look ahead. Let's just enjoy today."

Spoken like a typical Brazilian, Peggy thought in amusement. She had been here long enough to learn that the men in this country usually liked to live for the moment, under the impression that the future would take care of itself.

A burro, laden with great bunches of bananas, passed in the road, and Carlos called a greeting to the driver before he spoke again. "He used to be our gardener once upon a time," he explained idly. "Before Grandmother turned over the house to Mama and Papa."

"This Petrópolis house? It belonged to her?"

Carlos nodded. "You sound surprised."

Peggy shook her head. "I didn't mean to," she murmured, but Carlos continued to look at her quizzically.

"It's a shame there's such a language barrier," he said after a while. "You'd be interested in Granny. In her day she was a rather famous poet, you know."

"A poet?" Now there was no denying Peggy's astonishment.

Carlos nodded again. "In the romantic—or maybe I

should say classical—style. She wrote mostly about Bahia, which was her home."

"Oh?"

"I've never been to Salvador," said Carlos, as though he was thinking out loud, "but it must have more colonial flavor than any other city in Brazil. Grandmother says it is like a family portrait. She loved it there."

"Then why did she leave?" Peggy asked.

Carlos shrugged. "Her mother was a very aristocratic Sudanese. She was the favorite of a sugar baron, and after the abolition of slavery he moved here, to retire with what money he had left."

"You mean—your great-grandmother was a slave?"

"That's right," replied Carlos, quite unabashed, then added, "I suppose it seems remarkable to you."

"It does, rather," Peggy tried to keep her voice even and unemotional, but actually she was deeply shocked.

"It is a little unusual," Carlos admitted, "but of course *baianas* like my great-grandmother were unusual women. Actually, you know, there's not much pure Portuguese blood left in Brazil."

Peggy stared at an ant marching between grass blades at her feet. "That's what Daddy was saying," she remembered. That night at Mesbla—before she was seriously interested.

"About Granny's poetry," Carlos went on conversationally. "When you understand Portuguese a little better, I'd like to read you some. There's a sort of singing quality to her verse, but it doesn't hold up in translation, unfortunately."

Peggy stopped following the ant's progress. "That's too bad."

"Yes, it is." Oblivious of his companion's constraint, Carlos stretched languidly and added, "But then, of course, English poets don't translate very well into Portuguese, either." He chuckled in sudden amusement. "Can you imagine doing Poe, for instance? 'Quoth the Raven, "nevermore" ' would come out something like, *Disse o corvo, 'nunca mais.'* "

Laughing more from politeness than from amusement, Peggy got to her feet and brushed off her skirt. "Hadn't we better be getting along?" she asked. "That hill looks steep."

Actually, it was impossible to pedal a bicycle up the winding, rocky road, and for the rest of the way Peggy and Carlos walked, leaning on their handle bars when they stopped, every now and again, to rest.

The orchid farm was disappointing, because few specimens were in bloom, and the rows of plants with their spiky green leaves looked as bedraggled as Peggy was beginning to feel. Her legs ached from the unaccustomed climb, her skirt—so much less sensible than shorts for bicycling!—clung damply to her thighs, and only the pleasure of being with Carlos sustained her on the hazardous ride back down the hill.

Stones bounced from under the bicycle wheels, dogs yapped at Peggy's heels, goats scampered out of her path, and the brake was almost useless.

For a few seconds, as her bicycle careered down a road leading to the park, Peggy was afraid that she would completely lose control, but Carlos, whooping with unrestrained laughter, made the predicament funny instead of terrifying. He managed to reach the square before she did, and was ready to grab her and lift her off the bike, which finally came to rest with a clatter on the cobblestones several feet away from them.

"And here I thought you were the athletic type!" he teased. "What happened?"

"Brakes," Peggy gasped through her relieved giggles. "There just aren't any on that bike!"

Children riding around the park in donkey carts turned to look curiously at the red-haired girl and the abandoned bicycle, but Peggy was unaware of their stares. Once again, through the strange alchemy Carlos could exercise, she was under his spell, smiling up at him with a devotion so strangely overwhelming that it brought back the bloom to the day.

"I'm thirsty. How about a *guaraná?*"

"I'd love one."

Together Carlos and Peggy crossed to a refreshment stand, together stood and sipped the cool amber liquid, together looked with pleasure at the hoop-rolling children and their nursemaids, at the patiently waiting ponies, at the empty grandstand.

"Happy?" Carlos asked.

"Very."

"So am I."

Bells rang in a church tower. A clock chimed. "I suppose we should be getting back," Peggy said regretfully. "It must be noon."

On the terrace, Cleo and Guida were seated opposite one another at a small table, playing a two-handed game of cards. They looked up in welcome when Peggy and Carlos appeared, and Cleo asked, "How were the orchids? Didn't you bring any home?"

"There weren't many in bloom," reported Carlos, while Peggy realized that he had fallen into a trap.

Cleo simply raised a carefully plucked eyebrow. "There never are—are there—at this season?"

Dona Plácida, coming out of the dining-room door, paused for a moment, listening, and Peggy found herself flushing uncontrollably. "I think I'll go change for lunch," she murmured, excusing herself. "It was quite a warm ride."

The next day, when Carlos suggested another expedition *à deux*, this time to a museum, the former Emperor's palace, which housed the crown jewels, Dona Plácida suggested that by now Cleo was probably rested enough to go along too. She hired a carriage from one of a line of ancient vehicles waiting along the canal, and sent the four young people off with her blessing, smiling and waving from the gate as the carriage rattled away.

Carlos could scarcely conceal his disappointment, but Cleo was more affable than Peggy had ever found her before. She was full of information about the little resort city, and seemed to be especially anxious for

Peggy to enjoy herself. In the palace, where they all had to don felt slippers at the door, she scuffed around at the North American girl's side, taking her from room to room with a remarkable show of interest.

Abandoned to his sister's company, Carlos sulked. He made cutting remarks about the Emperor's taste in jewelry, yawned openly at the paintings, and looked scornfully at the palace furniture. Before the girls had finished their tour he went back outside, and amused himself by feeding a couple of flamboyant parrots, which were tethered to a garden perch.

Peggy was rather amused by his attitude, because it was obliquely flattering, but Guida was furious. "Really, Carlinhos, you could try to be a little better company!" she scolded. "Especially when we have guests."

Carlos made a grimace like a recalcitrant child, and Cleo laughed softly. "Men are allowed to be difficult, Guida," she murmured. "It's part of their charm."

Peggy considered the remark silly, but Carlos preened under such blandishment. Cozened and flattered, he began to enjoy the morning, and on the way back to the house he was his usual gay and ebullient self.

Walking upstairs with Cleo, while Guida ran out to the kitchen to announce that they were home, Peggy said forthrightly, "You certainly know how to handle that boy!"

Cleo smiled. "I should. I've known him since we were in prams."

"I keep forgetting that you're cousins," Peggy admitted.

"*Distant* cousins, dear."

Peggy laughed spontaneously, almost boisterously. There was something about this girl she liked, in spite of herself. Cleo pulled no punches. And suddenly Peggy realized that the situation had been reversed. Now it was Cleo who was considering *her* a threat!

And not only Cleo! As the week wore on, Dona Plácida as well seemed to become wary. In the evenings she made Cleo and Carlos stay home to play cribbage with herself and Dona Virgilia. Unwillingly, but with the politeness necessary under the circumstances, Peggy allowed herself to be dragged off to the *passeio* by Guida, who was still in a state of breathless excitement concerning her flirtation with Raymundo, and quite unaware that, to her house guest, the nocturnal ceremony had become a meaningless routine.

For the first time Peggy felt older than Guida—years older! The boys and girls strolling under the flower-laden trees, smiling at one another in a furtive, eyelash-fluttering way, were engaged in a game she had outgrown. To Peggy, the air was filled with a warm and aching longing, a tender love, but the *parque*, without Carlos, no longer interested her. Under duress, she accompanied Guida to the band concerts, and could scarcely wait to get back to the house.

But then she was inevitably disappointed. A game of cribbage was usually still in progress, and lasted until eleven o'clock, when Dona Plácida saw all of her

young charges off to bed. And each evening passed
without a chance to see Carlos alone.

It wasn't until Peggy's last night in Petrópolis that
opportunity again beckoned. Dona Virgilia, complain-
ing of a headache, did not appear at supper, but asked
for a tray to be sent to her room. Senhor Alfredo drove
up from Rio at sunset, and took his wife off to a dinner
party, so the young people were left in the house with
only Ignez, the children's old nurse, as chaperon.

Ignez installed herself firmly in a straight chair just
inside the terrace door, determined to be as vigilant
as her mistress apparently expected. But she had
ironed all day in the washhouse at the back of the
chácara, as the garden was called, then eaten more
than her share of rice and beans at supper. Within
fifteen minutes she was nodding, and in half an hour
her head had dropped to her ample bosom and she
was sound asleep.

Now it happened, as Carlos said later, that Cleo was
"hoist by her own petard." (He had been studying
Shakespeare and was full of apt quotations.) When
Peggy begged off, on the feeble excuse that she must
pack, Guida urged her cousin to come to the park with
her. Cleo, taking a leaf from Dona Virgilia's book,
claimed a splitting headache, and said regretfully that
she didn't feel like going out.

"You really should take some aspirin and go to bed,"
Guida suggested sympathetically, in spite of her disappointment.

Carlos seconded the motion, hurrying for the aspirin

bottle and practically propelling the reluctant Cleo
upstairs. "You'll want to feel better in the morning,"
he urged, and added something in a whisper that
Peggy couldn't hear.

For a second jealousy stabbed her, but then it became apparent that Carlos' ruse, whatever it might
be, was efficacious. Cleo went obediently to bed. Dis-
consolate, because she could lure nobody to the *passeio*, Guida followed, and Peggy, who by now had
forgotten all about her intended packing, was left
alone downstairs with Carlos.

They looked at each other in amused wonder,
scarcely able to believe their good fortune. Then Carlos proposed, in an undertone, "Let's go out to the
garden. It's a beautiful night!"

It didn't occur to Peggy to hesitate. Tiptoeing past
the sleeping Ignez, she led the way to the terrace like
a conspirator. "Oh, my goodness," she breathed, "I
didn't think I'd ever get another chance to see you
alone."

Carlos took her arm and led her out from under the
arbor across the grass to a screen of shrubbery. Then
he turned her around and took hold of her shoulders
and asked, as though, in spite of this revealing remark,
he needed to be convinced, "You do like me?"

"You know I do," Peggy whispered back. "I like
you very much." She caught her breath. "So much,
that sometimes it scares me to think that after school
closes you'll be going away."

Carlos didn't reply. He pulled her to him and put

his arms around her, standing very still for nearly a minute. Then he said a curious thing. "I wonder what it would be like to be free—really free, like you?"

"But you are free," Peggy said, raising her head from his shoulder. "You're a man! Men are much freer than girls."

"Are they?" Carlos seemed to be looking inward, asking himself the question rather than Peggy. "Are they? In the States, perhaps. Not in Brazil."

"I don't know what you mean," Peggy stumbled.

"Here everything is for the family," Carlos replied slowly. "Haven't you noticed the way Mama has been throwing Cleo at me all week?"

Of course Peggy had noticed, but she refused to admit it. Clenching her teeth, she waited for Carlos' next remark, but unexpectedly he held her off, rather roughly, by the elbows. "When am I going to see you again?"

His intensity made Peggy skittish. "Tomorrow morning, of course."

"But after that?"

"Whenever you come back to Rio."

Carlos frowned. "There's never enough time," he complained. "I've promised my uncle to work more often at the clinic. Then school will be starting, and—"

In the starlight Peggy could see a sudden gleam in Carlos' eyes. "And what?" she asked.

"Then there will be Carnival," he said. "You've never seen Carnival, have you? For three days, until midnight before Ash Wednesday, Rio goes completely mad. Maybe somehow we can plan to meet!"

But Peggy shook her head vigorously. "You don't know my mother! She was born and raised in Mobile, and during Carnival she'll keep me clutched as tight as a mother hen."

"But you'll go to parties!" Carlos protested. "And certainly to one of the big balls."

"I'm not at all sure," Peggy said wistfully. "And maybe they wouldn't be the same parties." Annoyed that they had reached such an inconvenient roadblock, she added rather sharply, "Which leaves us exactly where we started, on the beach."

Carlos chuckled softly and shook his head. "Not on the beach. In the cafeteria, remember? And then at Mesbla. I'll never forget the way you looked that night."

"And I'll never forget the orchid," Peggy said tremulously. All of a sudden she couldn't bear the thought of saying good-by to Carlos tomorrow morning. Even with Cleo complicating things, it had been a wonderful week.

Chapter 13

Peggy came up to the last green at Gavea, and got out her putter. Becky, who was walking around with her for the exercise, went over and plucked the flag out of the hole, then stood holding it while Peggy took casual aim and missed an easy putt.

"You weren't really looking," Becky accused, with the frankness of a good friend. "What's the matter with you today?"

Peggy shrugged. "It's funny about golf. You have to care."

"You have to care about *anything*," Becky said sententiously.

Peggy picked up her ball, stripped off her golf gloves, and said, "Come on, I'll get us something cool to drink."

"Not *guaraná*," said Becky. "I'm sick of the stuff."

"Orangeade? Pineapple juice?"

"Yes, *abacaxí*," replied Becky, then added belatedly, "please."

Seated at one of the little metal tables placed under

the shade trees off the club terrace, the two girls
waited for a boy to bring their drinks. Beyond them
the fairways stretched, green and empty, to the knobby
mountains. It was almost noon.

"You know," said Becky, taking out her lipstick and
repairing her make-up, "actually I'll be glad when
school starts. I'm getting bored."

"I'll be glad too," admitted Peggy, thinking of
Carlos. She had seen him twice this past week, but
each time at the clinic, where she was now employed
in so many tasks that there was not a free moment to
exchange more than an occasional word. Hurrying to
and from the examining room, as handsome as ever in
his blue work coat, he would glance at her tenderly
or in sly amusement, as the occasion warranted, but
he seemed distant and inaccessible. Only school could
change all that.

"Why do you suppose he didn't come to our picnic
last Saturday?" Becky asked unexpectedly.

"Who?"

"Carlos, of course."

"I don't know. Maybe he was busy."

"With Cleo?"

It was a thought Peggy had kept pushing to the
back of her mind. "How should I know?"

"Don't be snippy," Becky said with a grin. "*I'd*
worry about it too."

Peggy bent her head and put her lips to her straw,
so that Becky couldn't see her eyes. She was only too
aware that, so far as Dona Plácida was concerned, her

own position had altered. It was as simple as ABC, actually. Peggy had been invited to Petrópolis as Guida's friend and, as such, accepted cordially. Then Cleo had appeared, and with her coming the interest Carlos showed in the North American girl had become clearly defined. This changed the picture. Peggy became the outsider once more, the stranger, the foreigner. The Brazilian family folded its leaves like a sensitive plant at her lightest touch. It was perfectly obvious.

But it was also ridiculous. Carlos was eighteen years old, no child to be told what girl he should take to a party. He was almost a man, ready to go away to college next year, then on to medical school, where the Almeidas would have no hold on him. Or would they? She remembered his remark about not being free, but she couldn't figure it out, either then or now.

Peggy swallowed angrily, and her straw struck air instead of liquid at the bottom of the glass, emitting a sound that Tobey would have described as a "razzberry."

Becky leaned forward on her elbows. "You know, that very first day at school I tried to warn you off," she said. "Don't you remember, in the lunchroom?"

Peggy shook her head.

"I told you Cleo and Carlos were 'kissin' cousins.' "

"Well, I happen to know they're not," Peggy flared rebelliously. "He doesn't even like her. He says his family is trying to crowd him."

Becky didn't answer, but she looked irritatingly

wise, and Peggy remembered, in a flash back so vivid that she seemed to be reliving the scene, the moment when Carlos, on her last night in Petrópolis, had gone over to whisper something in Cleo's ear. It must have been a promise of some kind, which certainly pleased Cleo, because she immediately became amenable. At the time Peggy had been curious, but in the garden later she had completely forgotten to ask Carlos what ruse he had employed.

Stirring the leftover ice in her glass with the limp-tipped straw, Peggy sat in silence too, until Becky suddenly pushed back her chair with a mirthless chuckle. "I'm not trying to interfere, Peggy," she said. "I just don't want you to get hurt, and I don't think you understand the solidarity of these Brazilian families."

"Well, for Pete's sake, I'm not trying to *marry* Carlos. I'm not even wearing his pin. It's just that I want to see him once in a while. Is it wrong to like a boy?"

"No," said Becky. "But it can be dangerous to like a Brazilian boy too much."

"You sound like your own grandmother," Peggy scolded. "Oh, come on, let's go swimming. We've talked enough."

The girls walked back to the bathhouses, changed, and came out to the pool. Becky slipped into the cool water from the side, but Peggy went to the diving board and executed a clean and competent jackknife, coming up a few yards from Tobey, who was sitting on the coping kicking his heels.

"Hi. What's the matter with you?" asked his sister. "You look unhappy."

"I haven't got anything to do," Tobey replied.

"You're swimming, aren't you?" suggested Peggy. "What do you want, egg in your beer?"

The moment she had spoken she realized how disagreeable she must sound, using words borrowed from a slang expression of her father's, and in a tone choked with her own frustration. Then, to add to her dismay, she saw two tears roll slowly down her brother's cheeks.

Tobey's face didn't change expression. He didn't cry childishly, bursting into sudden fury as he sometimes did. He simply let the tears take their inevitable course, not even bothering to brush them away.

Contrite, Peggy pulled herself up to the coping. "I'm sorry, honey. Tell me about it. What's wrong?"

"I haven't got anybody to play with," Tobey said. "Swimming's no fun when you're alone."

"Of course it isn't!" Peggy agreed sympathetically. "Nothing's any fun when you're alone." She looked around the pool rather frantically for a familiar eight-year-old face, but there was none. Becky was standing in the shallow end talking to an acquaintance, a trio of ten-year-old girls were splashing one another under the diving board, but Tobey's age group was not represented at all.

"Where is everybody?" she asked.

"Jack's gone to the mountains, Tim is visiting his grandmother in the States, Bill is away somewhere—I don't know where," said Tobey, giving his sister a run-down of his North American acquaintances. "Ernesto's home, but Mommy says I can't bring him out here to the pool. Peggy, why doesn't Mommy like Ernie? Why won't she let me? Do you know?"

Peggy knew only too well, and while she should have been prepared for this question, it still came as a shock. It smote her like a physical blow, from which she had to recoil and, in recoiling, make some kind of answer.

Because of her own experience during these past months, she could no longer bring herself to brush her brother off with an easy lie. She realized, with a compassion that was as overwhelming as it was unexpected, that Tobey's problem was just as important to him as her romance with Carlos was to her. He deserved an honest answer.

And here he sat, waiting for her to reply, trusting her, or he wouldn't have spoken. "Why won't she let me? Do you know?"

"Yes, I know," Peggy said. "But I don't know if I can explain to you, because you're awfully young to understand."

"You could try," Tobey suggested sensibly.

"Well, here it is, then. Mother doesn't like you to play with Ernie because he's a colored boy."

"He is not!" Tobey flared. "He's a Brazilian."

"He's a Brazilian, too, but his skin is dark," Peggy

went on courageously, although her throat felt tight and her hands were clammy.

"But in Brazil that doesn't matter! Daddy said so. You heard him!" Tobey accused.

"Mother," said Peggy sadly, "is thinking of the time when we go home." Now that she had started, she had to go on and explain. "Back home it would make things very hard for Mother if you had friends who were colored."

"Even if they were nice boys?"

"Even if they were nice boys."

Tobey whirled on his sister like a little wildcat. "But that's wrong!" he cried, without caring who heard him. "That's wicked. You know it is."

Peggy couldn't meet the child's accusing eyes. "It is wrong," she admitted, as she stared blindly at the rippling water, "but it isn't anything Mother can help."

"She should try!" flared Tobey.

"Yes, she should. But there are lots of reasons why she doesn't, why she feels she can't. These are things I can't explain to you because I don't understand them any too well myself. Honestly."

"O.K."

Peggy took a deep breath. "The South has always been split into colored people and white people," she said. "You know the signs on places. But in Washington they've declared that things have got to change, and maybe they will. Maybe you and I can help make them."

"What can we do? That's silly."

"Not so silly. We can do what we're doing now—talk about this thing, think about it, see if we can find a way to make things better for everybody."

Tobey gave a deep sigh, as though he'd digested as much as he could handle today. "Anyway," he said, just before he slid off the coping into the water, "Mommy's stupid—plain stupid!—about Ernie!"

As she watched her brother swim away, Peggy knew exactly how he felt, but it was impossible to shoulder all of his problems. She could barely struggle along with her own.

At that moment Becky floated up. "Stop looking so glum," she commanded, as though Peggy had left her only a moment before. "Let's go get a sandwich or something. It's lunch time."

Lunch time, dinnertime, and then breakfast time on a new day. A week passed, and school opened. Now, no longer a stranger, Peggy looked on a shy and diffident "new girl" with a sense of pity, but she was so caught up in her own affairs that there seemed to be no time to be more than casually kind.

Carlos and the rest of the senior class had the air of racers going into the last lap. They talked credits and colleges and advanced placement and the results of college boards. Nevertheless, Carlos managed to seek Peggy out on the very first morning of the new term and to slip her a note as she was going into the classroom where Portuguese was taught.

She read it under cover of her desk top. "Dear Peggy," he had written, in a large and casual masculine scrawl. "I want to see you, but I'm being kept pretty busy. Can't we make a date for Carnival next week? Surely you can get away for an evening. We could have a wonderful time!"

Peggy was gratified by such interest, but disturbed by a suggestion which she knew would never have been made to a Brazilian girl. "I told you Mother wouldn't let me," she wrote back impatiently, "and I'm not the type who plays hooky. Can't you dream up something more *possible?*"

It took a full day to get this message to Carlos, and in the meantime something more possible fell right out of the blue Rio sky. Miss Margaret Cullen Jamison, along with her parents, was invited to the ball at the Copacabana Palace by the Andersons, who were fellow members of the Gavea Golf Club.

There was no question about their acceptance. "I think it sounds delightful," Mrs. Jamison said at once. "Everyone says the party at the Copa is one of the nicest in the city. It should be something like the balls at the Athelstan Club, back home in Mobile."

"Will we wear fancy dress?" asked Mr. Jamison a trifle dubiously. "I hate costume affairs."

"I'll have to ask Ruth Anderson," his wife said. "Maybe you can get away with black tie. But I'm sure Peggy will want to go masked. It's half the fun."

Peggy's heart leaped, and at once she thought of Carlos. Here might be an opportunity—

"Won't you, honey?" her mother was inquiring.

"Yes, I guess so. But it's awfully late to dream up a

clever costume, isn't it? Some of the girls at school have been working on theirs for months."

Indeed, coincident to the new school term and the return of cooler weather, all of Rio had acquired a holiday air. Even in the *favela*, when Peggy had gone to the clinic for the last time, there had been a feeling of Carnival in the atmosphere. Samba music blared from the tipsy doorway of an adobe hut; sewing machines whirred; a naked child ran down the hill trailing a yard of tinsel; and a dusky beauty, dressed in a gaudy drum-majorette costume, preened in front of an admiring group of neighbors.

Brought back to the present by her mother saying, "Let me see. Get up, sweetie. Walk around, and I'll just think a minute," Peggy obeyed automatically. Mrs. Jamison regarded her daughter through eyes that considered all the possibilities of their wardrobes. Then she suddenly snapped her fingers. "I've got it! Your green leotard. There are wonderful shops down by the docks that sell cured leathers. With your long legs—"

"With my long legs, what?" Peggy asked, when her mother hesitated.

"There's no doubt about it," Mrs. Jamison said, as though she had never paused, "you'll make a delightful Robin Hood. A tan leather jerkin, a little felt cap with a feather. There's a man who sells feathers in the *feira*, right next to the booth with toads' teeth and all those *macumba* things."

Peggy laughed, because she very much doubted that

toads had teeth, but the idea of being Robin Hood appealed to her, even though it was a boy's role. The costume sounded romantic and becoming. Because, as a matter of fact, she did have good legs!

The next day at school she sent a brief note to Carlos. "My parents have accepted an invitation to a ball at the Copa Palace," she wrote, and named the date. "I'm included. Shall I tell you what I'm to wear?"

Carlos sped a note in return, pressing it into Peggy's hand as they passed in the hall. "Darling," he wrote, "of course tell me! We'll be at the Copa, too, that night, so it makes everything great."

Although at school there was no real need for such conspiracy, Peggy continued to indulge Carlos in his desire to play this game of passing notes back and forth. She treasured his scrawled messages, containing such wonderful signals of his attachment as the word "darling" and a daring "x x x" inscribed beneath his name. He had never once used such endearments in real life, but on paper he apparently felt free to let himself go.

All over Rio, Carnival fervor began to reach a fever pitch. Even Tobey was affected by it, partly because it seemed so remarkable that no sooner had school started, than everyone was to be let out for a three-day vacation.

Coming home from the office at night, Mr. Jamison would report all sorts of preparations on the Avenida Rio Branco downtown. "Rio's excitement over Carnival songs beats Brooklyn's interest in the Dodgers when I was a kid Tobey's age," he announced one evening. "Everybody who can hit a lick on a tin can is out in the streets thumping a tune."

An important ceremony at the beginning of Carnival would be the awarding of prizes out of the city treasury for the top songs. Judging by ear, a committee of representative citizens was already circulating all over town, deciding which numbers seemed to be getting the biggest play from wandering bands, from shufflers and chanters. At the Escola Americana pupils sang Carnival songs in the halls, whistled them on the playgrounds, and thumped them out on the old piano in the gym.

Peggy found herself humming the high favorite, one that was being shrilled from trumpets at every *bistro* along the Avenida Atlântica and played on every radio and by every café orchestra. Carnival was contagious. The waves, rolling up on the beach, no longer whispered, *"Whoosh,"* but murmured, *"Carnival is coming,"* with a long sweet sweep.

Jacinta announced that she would take three days off. There was no question of asking for permission. From the Amazon to Rio Grande do Sul, nobody worked during Carnival, except the help employed at the big hotels. Business offices, schools, museums, and libraries, all shut down tight, and the entire nation embarked on a wild and wonderful spree, with Rio's festival the biggest and best of all.

The last afternoon at school there was little studying done. Teachers as well as pupils seemed to be in-

fected with the incipient gaiety. Carlos, knowing that
Peggy would be at the Copacabana Palace ball dressed
as Robin Hood, refused to reciprocate by telling her
how he could be recognized.

"That isn't fair!" Peggy objected, provoked. "I told
you!"

But Carlos only laughed and teased her with a
scrambled answer. "Maybe I'll just wear a domino.
But watch for a wolf! Or an Eskimo. No, that would
be hot, wouldn't it? I'll have to find a costume my
personality will shine through."

Peggy stalked off in pretended annoyance, but she
had to admit that Carlos' secrecy heightened her anticipation. By Carnival's opening day, when her father
took the family down to his office to watch the crowds
in the Avenida Rio Branco, the hub of the ceremonies,
she was counting the hours until the big night.

The boulevard's black-and-white mosaic sidewalks
were hidden by a throng as thick as a heaving rug.
Brassy, brazen, overdressed, underdressed, all Rio
seemed to be moving to the blare of trumpets. Mil-
lions of feet were beating time, shuffling, and jumping
to coarse but compelling rhythms. Peggy stood looking
down, half-repelled, half-entranced. She had never
seen grown people shake off convention with such
utter abandon. It was shocking, but in a way it was
wonderful.

Every once in a while the confusion resolved itself
into something like a parade. The big clubs, called
Democráticos, Tenentes do Diabo, and *Fenianos,* all

had elaborate floats, planned in secret and constructed over a long period of time. "They're competing for a prize," Peggy explained to Tobey, who didn't take time to listen. He had been given a supply of paper streamers, and was busy pelting the passing throng.

"How many people *are* there in Rio?" asked Tobey curiously, as he leaned against the window sill.

"About three million," his father said.

"And are they *all* out there?"

"All but a few convicts in solitary, the permanently bedridden, and—I suppose—Jacinta's North American missionary friends," replied Mr. Jamison with a grin.

The floats passed, and the crowd milled in the street once more, young and old singing and dancing together in groups called *blocos*. The gaiety was unforced, and there seemed to be little drinking. "That's because only beer and champagne—one too filling and the other too expensive—are allowed to be sold," Mr. Jamison said.

The air was laden, however, with a sweet smell, which Peggy found vaguely familiar. "That's called *lança-perfume*," her father said, "but actually it's ether. They squirt a solution of it from water pistols and sniff it from damp handkerchiefs, I'm told."

"How revolting," Mrs. Jamison murmured, but she didn't seem unduly distressed. Like Tobey, she looked on the scene below as on a brilliant musical comedy, with ingenious decorations and music that was catchy, though loud.

A steel band came marching down the street, and to

Peggy it seemed to be echoing a rhythm pounding in her brain. "Tomorrow night," the drummer was beating; "Tomorrow night," the cymbals were clanging. "Tomorrow night and Carlos and the Copacabana ball!"

She drew a long breath and clasped her hands tightly, wishing the hours would hurry, wondering how she could ever wait.

Chapter 14

The ball was to start at midnight and continue until dawn. Peggy had never been to such a late party, and she was desperately afraid she wouldn't be able to stay awake all night. Encouraged by her mother, she tried to sleep during the early part of the evening, but the noise in the street outside her window was so distracting that she could only lie with her eyes closed and will the hours to pass.

At eleven o'clock, shivering a little from anticipation, she started to dress, wriggling into the dark-green leotard and pulling the cleverly fashioned tan leather jerkin over her head. Then she teased and lacquered her hair into a stiff page-boy style, which she considered mildly masculine, and cocked a dashing green felt hat, flaunting an orange feather, well over one eye.

"You look straight out of Sherwood Forest," her father told her. "A robber baron par excellence."

"You look pretty neat yourself," Peggy replied, glad that her parent had been persuaded to add some Carnival accessories to his tuxedo. He was wearing a pair

of yellow gloves, carrying a flashlight, and had a bur-
glar's mask and a slouch hat, which made him look
like the fabled Jimmy Valentine.

Mrs. Jamison, who took an Alabama girl's delight in
Carnival but loved to be comfortable, was costumed in
a turn-of-the-century motoring outfit—long linen duster,
picture hat, and veil. She was so absorbed in getting her daughter and husband properly outfitted that
she almost forgot her goggles, which were to take the
place of the mask.

Peggy's domino was dark brown, and it covered
only her nose and eyes, yet she felt it disguised her
adequately. To strangers she hoped that her lacquered
hair would look like a wig. To Carlos, however, it
would be a certain means of identification.

Carlos! Her heart sang the name as the car pulled
up in the U-shaped drive of the Copacabana Palace,
already ankle deep in confetti and paper streamers.
Carlos! She peered in considerable trepidation at the
guests streaming through the hotel doors. Would they
ever find one another in this crowd?

A throng of Carnival marchers and street dancers
had stopped to watch the latest arrivals get out of their
cars. One swarthy father in a pirate's costume held a
two-year-old child high in his arms to give him a better
look. The baby was wearing nothing but a clown's
ruff and a pair of stained striped pants, but his shouts
of laughter were sure proof that he was enjoying being
out at midnight as much as anyone else.

Peggy impulsively blew the baby a kiss, which

brought a cheer from the amused crowd. Before she could reach the lobby she was sprinkled liberally with confetti and even squirted with *lança-perfume* by a juvenile prankster, but it was plain that it was all in fun.

The ballroom itself was ablaze with lights and bright with shimmering decorations. Great balloons hung from the ceiling and an orchestra was playing the new Carnival music, while dancers milled around the floor.

Instantly Peggy began to search for someone who might be Carlos. Her eyes discovered a court jester who was the right height but the wrong girth, a clown who was too short, a soldier with a busby who was too tall. As she made her way to the table the Andersons had reserved she was so busy discarding possibilities that she was unaware of the stir her own costume was causing. A good many of the glances that followed her progress belied the family's insistence that she made a convincing young man.

"I'm afraid you're going to be more of a success than we anticipated," her mother whispered to Peggy, as they wove in and out of the crowded tables. "But just behave very circumspectly and everything will be all right."

To be circumspect at this mad and merry ball was such an absurd idea that Peggy burst out laughing, but she patted her mother's arm and said, "I'll do my best." Then they were being greeted by their host and hostess, and introduced to several other guests at a big round table right on the edge of the dance floor.

The party was already in full swing, but instead of dancing in couples, which Peggy had expected, these masked dancers were moving around the floor counterclockwise, in groups of three, four, and even five. They were shuffling, jumping, singing, swinging, for all the world like the dancers in the streets, and the moment Peggy sat down a black-hatted gaucho tried to pull her to her feet and get her to join his group.

She smiled, but shook her head so vigorously that he laughed and moved away. "Goodness!" Peggy said. "This *is* different."

Mrs. Anderson, who was sitting on Peggy's left, nodded in agreement. "You see," she said, with the wisdom of a North American who had lived in Rio for several years, "a Carnival ball is a very liberal kind of ball. Many of the formalities are dispensed with, and it's quite all right for a boy to beckon or smile at you. This is just as much an invitation as if he came over and asked for permission to dance. If you smile back he'll come and take you by the hand—just like that. It makes everything terribly easy."

"But suppose you don't want to dance?" asked Peggy.

"Don't smile," replied her hostess, "until you see someone who looks attractive."

Oh, Carlos, come quickly! Peggy pleaded soundlessly. She felt timid and unsure of herself among all these strangers. If only she could see Carlos' familiar grin, feel the touch of his warm, strong hand.

Now she was no longer intrigued by the fact that

he had kept his costume secret. She wanted to be able to identify him at once among these groups of merry-makers surging around the floor in shifting patterns. The music was infectious. She wanted to get out there and be part of the fun!

Mr. Anderson, a bluff, hearty man, costumed in the medal-laden, beribboned full dress of an ambassador, began to urge the younger members of the party to accept the inviting eyes and outstretched hands of the passing dancers.

"Don't be afraid," he told Peggy, in a voice like a trombone. "We'll be vigilant chaperons."

"It isn't that," Peggy demurred, but she began to feel more and more impatient. She looked curiously at every long-limbed lad who passed, trying to penetrate his disguise, and her interest was rewarded by a good deal of attention. If Carlos was one of these, teasing her, she vowed she'd never forgive him, never! But at heart she knew that when he appeared she would be putty in his hands.

A trio danced past very close to Peggy's chair, and she pushed it back a little. Between an Arab sheik and a convincing Uncle Sam in striped trousers, cutaway, and star-decorated top hat, danced a diminutive girl in harem trousers and a nose veil. The Arab stretched out his hand pleadingly, but Peggy shook her head, then looked after the group with sudden curiosity. The girl *could* be Guida.

She waited for them to come by again, and this time Uncle Sam was on the outside, nearest Peggy. He stopped, made a sweeping bow, and with an authority that left her no time to refuse, pulled her to her feet and carried her into the surge of masqueraders. She still wasn't sure, so she went reluctantly, dragged along like a tail on a kite, the bells on the upturned toes of her Robin Hood slippers tinkling ineffectually in protest. She could sense rather than hear a ripple of amused laughter from the table she had left, and then she was lost in the maelstrom of dancers.

Neatly and swiftly, Uncle Sam pulled Peggy around to the inside, and the dancing girl caught her free hand and squeezed it.

"Guida?" Peggy asked timidly.

The girl's laughter was reply enough. Relief flooded over Peggy, and she turned to look up at Uncle Sam. "You might have told me!"

"You might have guessed!" complained Carlos. "I wore this costume just for you."

"Of course you did. I'm terribly stupid." Superficially Peggy was contrite, but her feet, beginning to step to the beat of the music, expressed her elation. She leaned forward to look beyond Guida to the Arabian sheik, and asked, in North American jargon, "Who he?"

Carlos roared with laughter, as he always did when Peggy became slangy, but Guida leaned close for a second and whispered in her ear, "Can't you guess that either?"

"Raymundo?" Peggy's lips framed the word silently. Guida nodded, her dark eyes, above the concealing nose veil, sparkling with delight. "He doesn't speak any English, so you'll have to practice your Portuguese."

As soon as the music stopped, Peggy was properly introduced to the tall Arabian. She murmured, *"Eu não falo português,"* after a few words of greeting, but Raymundo protested, and assured her that she spoke very well.

The orchestra launched into a traditional Carnival tune, and the dancing started again, to a step that was something—but not quite!—like a samba. Carlos, Raymundo, and Guida were all singing now.

> Viva Ze Pereira,
> que a ninguém faz mal,
> Viva Ze Pereira,
> No dia de Carnaval!

"Sing!" Carlos urged Peggy.

"I don't know the words."

Pronouncing the Portuguese very carefully, he sang directly to her, and she began to follow softly, then more confidently, as she was swept again and again around the floor. She was aware that her parents were watching her in amusement, but she didn't care. She was caught up in the rhythm of the dance, compelled to move to the strange tempo of the music. She was part of Carnival at last!

During an intermission Peggy brought the group

over to the table, but they lingered very briefly. It was a night during which young people wanted to be constantly on the move. When her feet began to cry for a brief rest Carlos led her out of the ballroom onto the broad stone terrace overlooking the sea, and she sat on a balustrade fanning herself with her hat. "That was really fun," she said.

"Was? Is! The ball is just beginning. We'll dance 'til dawn."

Peggy wriggled her toes, glad that she wasn't wearing high heels. "Goody."

The music from the ballroom was muted but still insistent. "It's like an African dance, an Indian ceremonial, and a Portuguese love song, all rolled into one," Peggy murmured.

"You know, Pegeen, you can be very perceptive," Carlos said. "But let's not talk about the music. Let's talk about you. I haven't told you how marvelous you look—like a young boy, sort of."

Peggy put back her head and laughed. "I'm glad you added 'sort of.'"

Carlos touched her jerkin. "Real leather!"

Peggy nodded. "We found it in a store down by the docks." But the costume no longer interested her. She was feeling unexpectedly daring. "Carlos—"

"Yes?"

"Do you know what I'd like to do?"

"Tell me."

"I'd like to slip away for a few minutes and go out

into the street crowd. Just to get the feeling of being among the people. Do you think we could?"

"Certainly," said Carlos, tilting his Uncle Sam hat at a rakish angle. " 'Your wish is my command.' "

They ran down the marble stairs, through the lobby, and out into the Avenida Atlântica like two truants escaping from school. Carlos turned toward the city, and they walked with the crowd, watching the antics of the celebrants with fascination. There were jugglers, organ-grinders, flag-bearers, horn blowers, drummers, even a group engaged in twirling striped umbrellas to the rhythm of their dancing feet. This sweaty, hoarse, irrepressible crowd was as different from the revelers in the ballroom as the children of the *favelas* were different from those attending the American School.

Occasionally Peggy grasped Carlos' arm in an instinctive appeal for protection against what seemed to be an unbridled mob, but actually the people were astonishingly considerate and mannerly. When they reached the Avenida Princesa Isabel, leading into the center of the city, Peggy tugged at Carlos' sleeve. "I guess we'd better go back," she said. "Thank you for bringing me."

"Let's walk on the beach, then," Carlos proposed, and led her across the boulevard and over serpentine pavement to the sand, then down to the tide line, where the sounds of saturnalia were muted.

"This is something you should never be doing," he warned her lightly. "Walking alone on the beach with a boy at three o'clock in the morning! Aren't you ashamed?"

"Not in the least," Peggy replied candidly. "You're not just any boy. You're a very particular boy. And if I didn't trust you I wouldn't be here."

"Forthright. That's the word for you, my sweet. But I like it," Carlos said. "I like it, and I like you. I wish I could tell you how much."

"You have—without words," Peggy whispered.

Carlos tucked her hand through his arm once more, and drew her close, so that they could walk in step slowly. "I wish you were a Brazilian," he sighed, "but then, of course, you wouldn't be you."

"Oh, yes I would be!" Peggy insisted.

"No, darling, no," Carlos muttered under his breath. "You'd be quite different. How old are you, Peggy?"

"Nearly seventeen."

"Then you wouldn't be thinking about college; you'd be thinking about marriage. You'd be planning a big wedding in the cathedral, and you'd be wondering whether you might have a dozen children, or maybe only nine."

"That doesn't sound so unattractive," said Peggy, cocking her head and looking out over the shimmering sea.

"But it sounds several years away," said Carlos realistically.

"Well—"

"Enjoy the moment, Peggy!" cried Carlos, suddenly dropping her hand and spreading his arms. "Enjoy the here and now." He picked her up and swung her around and around until her head began to swim and she gasped, "Put me down!"

"The point is," said Carlos, sobering, "you're free. You were born free."

"You sound like a broken phonograph record," Peggy accused.

"You mean I said the same thing in Petrópolis?"

"Yes."

"But you didn't understand then, and you don't now. Just remember—someday—that I tried to tell you something important." He pulled her against him and began to stroke her hair.

But Peggy edged back. "You act as though we were —we were—"

"Don't say it," Carlos whispered. "Just remember that for me there has never been anyone like you. There never will be! No matter what happens, please remember that."

"Carlos—" Peggy's heart was beating so loudly that she felt she should shout above the hammering, but actually she spoke barely above a whisper. "Carlos— do you think we're in love?"

He held her very close, but he didn't speak for a long moment. "A little, my darling," he said finally. "Maybe more than a little."

"It's wonderful, isn't it?" Peggy asked.

"It's very wonderful," Carlos said soberly. "I wish we belonged to one world."

"But we do!" Peggy exclaimed. "Why, New York is only eight hours away from Rio by jet."

"How very true!" Carlos laughed rather shakily, then looked in quiet desperation at the moon, swinging high over the water. "Come on!" he said suddenly. "Let's run. Everybody—and especially my mother—will be wondering where we've gone."

Chapter 15

She was in love! It was the first thought Peggy had when she awakened the next morning, surprised that the raucous sounds of Carnival continued in the Avenida. As far as she was concerned, the climax had been reached, the party should be over, the Cariocas might as well take off their costumes, clean up the streets, and go to church.

For Peggy, this Carnival would be a lasting memory, but now she wanted time to collect herself, time to think, time to dream of the day when Carlos and she need no longer kiss good-by. I'd like a little place in the hills above Gavea, she thought romantically. A villa with a view, an avocado tree, and a bougainvillaea vine over the roof. Senhora Carlos Almeida. How lovely it sounded, how right! Senhora Almeida, formerly Miss Margaret Cullen Jamison of Charlotte, North Carolina, U.S.A. With her picture in the papers, and Laurette sending her a sterling-silver dish for a wedding present, and everybody wishing her happiness.

Of course it wasn't going to come to pass immediately. Carlos still had to go to college, and then on to medical school. Peggy began to count the years on her fingers, stopped at six, and began to revise her plans. A little apartment near Harvard in Cambridge, Massachusetts—maybe a converted carriage house or something equally exciting—and all sorts of bright young people dropping in for Sunday brunch. That would do for a beginning, but eventually, inevitably, she saw herself back in Rio, developing into Guida's idea of a smart young matron, lunching at the Modern Art Museum or at the French Embassy roof-top restaurant, happily receiving compliments on the work of her husband, the famous young surgeon. Oh, what a wonderful life it would be!

When school opened again the next day Peggy was still drifting through a dream, her feet scarcely touching the floor. She slipped into her seat in French class, quite unprepared for Guida's quick question. "What did you think of him?"

"Who?" Peggy asked stupidly.

"Raymundo, of course."

"Oh, I thought he was terribly nice," Peggy replied politely, although privately she considered the boy rather pallid, quite out of character in his sheik's robe.

"I think he's wonderful," Guida breathed, resting her chin on her cupped hands. "Mama liked him too. She says we can invite him to the house sometime— sometime soon."

Guida's naïve delight was touching. Peggy smiled

and murmured, "That's marvelous!" but unfortunately the mention of Dona Plácida recalled the one moment during the ball that had been less than utterly perfect. When she and Carlos had returned from the beach he had led her over to his family's table at the far end of the ballroom and she had had an opportunity to pay her respects.

"*Boa noite,* Peggy," Dona Plácida had said, with a polite smile, but both her voice and her expression had lacked warmth. She turned immediately to her son and, with some asperity, said in Portuguese, "I have been wondering why you left the floor."

"For a moment only, *Mamãe,*" Carlos had replied, with a grin intended to be endearing.

"A long moment," Dona Plácida retorted, again in Portuguese, while Peggy stood by uncomfortably, rather wishing that she couldn't understand.

Oh, well—by Brazilian standards they had been naughty, Peggy supposed, and she as well as Carlos had been punished in this manner. But that eventually Dona Plácida would learn to accept her gave her not the slightest pause. Far more important would be her own mother's reaction to the Almeidas, and especially to Dona Virgilia!

This was a problem which she had pushed to the back of her mind and which floated to the surface, only because she found French class dull and had time to sit and cogitate. When the forty-five minutes were over she decided not to cross bridges before she came to them, and told herself that after another six months in Brazil her mother's attitude toward the color question was bound to change.

None of this did she actually believe, but she was not in a mood for a realistic analysis of the situation. The question uppermost in her mind was whether she might meet Carlos in the hall between this class and the next, and whether his eyes would tell her, without words, that he treasured as much as she those early-morning moments on the starlit beach.

But Carlos was not around, either that day or the next. Guida offered the information that he was taking examinations. "I'm not sure what," she added. "There are so many different types required for North American colleges these days that I get them all mixed up."

"Will Raymundo be going to the States to college?" Peggy asked casually, and was surprised to see an expression of concern cross Guida's face.

"I doubt it," she replied after a moment. "He'll probably go to the University of Brazil." Then, in a burst of confidence, she added, "Oh, Peggy, I *do* wish Papa wouldn't insist on sending me away for four years. Why, by the time I'm through with school I'll be a dried-up old woman of twenty-one. By then all my friends will be married, with three or four children!"

"Not *all* your friends! Surely you're exaggerating."

"Almost all," insisted Guida. "And I'm so afraid Raymundo isn't the type of person who will want to wait."

Astonished, Peggy said, "But you scarcely know him. Aren't you jumping the gun a bit?"

"Jumping the gun?" Guida was puzzled by the unfamiliar slang. "What is that?"

"Getting ahead of yourself. You don't know Raymundo one quarter as well as I know—as I know Carlos, for instance," Peggy admitted, because she had gone too far to stop.

"Oh, but that's different," Guida said instantly. "We know Raymundo's family. He'll be coming to call on me now, and the way is open for things to be arranged."

"Arranged? What do you mean?"

Guida stared at Peggy as though they were suddenly worlds apart. "Here it's different, I guess, from the States. I mean I just can't marry *anybody*. It would have to be someone my parents approved of, naturally."

To Peggy it didn't seem natural at all. It seemed spineless. It took all the zest and unexpectedness out of romance. Raymundo, inspected, discussed, and approved by the Almeidas, became about as glamorous as an old shoe.

"Like Cleo," Guida was rattling along. "For years it has been sort of taken for granted that Carlos and Cleo will marry someday. The families are very close. It would be the most natural thing in the world."

Again the word "natural" slapped Peggy like a wet towel across her face. Yet for once she was speechless, because this was no time to tell Guida that Carlos didn't even like Cleo, that everything was changed— gloriously changed! Guida would find out in due time.

Carlos was not—thank heaven!—the same type as Ray-mundo.

"Of course, with Carlos going to the States to college—" Peggy started, then let the obvious conclusion hang in the air.

On Friday, at the close of school, Mrs. Jamison picked her daughter up in the car, so that they could go to the dressmaker together. It was one of those seasons in which skirt lengths were changing almost faster than even the most assiduous reader of fashion magazines could keep up with them. The back seat of the little automobile was stacked with dresses to be altered, and it would be necessary to stand endlessly for pinnings, so the dressmaker could make the necessary adjustments required by style.

Peggy was agreeable, but not enthusiastic. Fittings bored her, important though they were. On the way downtown her mother chattered amiably about a hand-knit sweater she had seen. Now that the weather was a little cooler, she thought she'd stop and pick up some yarn and do a little knitting herself.

"As a matter of fact, we have time right now," she said, pulling into a parking space along the Avenida Copacabana. "There's a marvelous place in this block —a shop all the Cariocas use—that's supposed to be especially good."

Peggy accompanied her mother down the street with a certain amount of interest. She could use a new cardigan herself—a white one preferably—which she could throw over her shoulders on a cool night. She visualized herself coming out of a motion picture with Carlos and flinging it around her shoulders casually, or—better yet—handing it to him to adjust.

"Here it is. *Loja Conchita*," Mrs. Jamison was saying. "Right here."

Peggy stepped ahead to push open the glass door that led from the street, when she unexpectedly found herself face to face with Dona Plácida, who, along with the elderly Dona Virgilia, was just coming out of the store.

"*Boa tarde*, Peggy," said Dona Plácida with equanimity, although Peggy drew back in an embarrassment she couldn't control. While Peggy held the door, the *Senhora* helped her mother-in-law negotiate the rather awkward step down, then waited to be introduced.

Peggy was utterly appalled that this situation, which she had so persistently dreaded, should have caught her off guard. Too stunned to dare look into her mother's face, she faltered ineptly through her presentation, first of Dona Plácida, then of Carlos' diminutive dark-skinned grandmother.

Dona Virgilia peered at Mrs. Jamison through her keen little eyes, set like black buttons in her wrinkled nut-brown face. She murmured a courteous greeting in Portuguese, then smiled in a friendly fashion at Peggy, quite unaware that she might be the cause of the flush that had mounted to the roots of the girl's hair.

Mrs. Jamison maintained her poise with difficulty. She thanked Senhora Plácida for entertaining her

daughter so generously in Petrópolis, and murmured
that she had tried to express her appreciation in a note
but was glad that now she could thank her personally.

To this rather effusive speech Dona Plácida bowed
in graceful acknowledgment, but she didn't linger.
The civilities over, it was obvious that she was anxious
to get Dona Virgilia into the waiting car.

A moment later Peggy and her mother were inside
the shop, with the door closed behind them. Mrs.
Jamison didn't mince words. She grasped her daughter's arm and asked, in shocked disbelief, "Did you
say that was Carlos' *grandmother?*"

Peggy nodded mutely, then found her voice, and
bristling with defiance, replied, "Yes, it is."

"Well," said Mrs. Jamison. "Well!" She leaned
weakly against the counter and regarded the clerk,
who came to help her, with no remembrance at all of
what she had come about.

"You were looking for yarn, Mother."

"Oh, yes, yarn. For a sweater—a pull-over. Something in a Shetland perhaps."

"*Desculpe.*"

"She doesn't speak English, Mother." Peggy translated the request into halting Portuguese, and eventually the transaction was completed.

Back in the car, Peggy gathered her forces and sat
tense and ready for the explosion she felt was bound
to come. Her mother, however, didn't say a word. In
silence she got out at the dressmaker's, abstractedly

stood for the fittings, waited in turn for her daughter, and in deep preoccupation drove home.

Having lined up her arguments and readied herself for combat, Peggy felt almost indignant that she was not attacked. The last thing for which she had been prepared was this distracted refusal to face the issue and talk it out.

The apartment door was opened by Jacinta, who asked at once, "Is Tobey with you, *Senhora?*"

"No," replied Mrs. Jamison, as though she was making an effort to refocus her thoughts. "Hasn't he come home from school?"

Peggy walked to the window. "Shall I go down to the beach and look for him?" she asked quickly.

"He isn't on the beach," said Jacinta. "I've been there."

Anxious to be placating, because she realized that her mother was already deeply disturbed, Peggy said, "Well, maybe he stopped off at a friend's house."

Mrs. Jamison dropped her handbag on a chair. "What friend?" she asked sharply.

Just then the door buzzer sounded, and Peggy hurried across the room, saying, "Probably that's Tobey now."

But it was a florist's delivery man, holding out a square white box. "Senhorita Margaret Jamison?" he asked, hesitating over the English names.

"Yes," Peggy started, then corrected herself. "*Sim. Obrigado, senhor.*"

She took the box rather reluctantly, carried it to

the dining-room table, and opened it. A sixth sense had told her what she would find—a white orchid—accompanied by a sealed envelope, across which her nickname was scrawled in Carlos' familiar hand.

At any other time Peggy would have been bubbling with delight, tearing open the flap to read the message inside, but this evening she tucked the envelope secretively into her skirt pocket. "Isn't it pretty? Carlos must think it's my birthday or something," she murmured inanely, feeling that the timing was all wrong, wanting to accept happily this token of Carlos' affection, but wishing it had come on another day.

There the box lay, with the blossom cradled on its shredded tissue, for all the world like a bird in a nest. Peggy stood staring at it for a long moment, then realized that her mother was staring too. She tried to smile, but although her lips moved obediently to a signal from her brain, there was no warmth in her expression. Suddenly she turned, walked quickly into the bathroom, and locked the door.

Now, like a sleepwalker, she drew out the envelope and turned it over, running a fingernail under the flap and taking out the white card inside. "I've got to see you, Peggy," Carlos had written, his letters boldly formed and impatient. "Meet me at the Modern Art Gallery, near the side door, tomorrow morning at ten o'clock. Please come alone."

Peggy leaned against the closed door, suddenly weak and wretched. This wasn't like Carlos. What could be wrong?

She walked over to the sink and washed her hands, stared at her face in the mirror as though she were encountering a stranger, and applied fresh lipstick as if she were arming herself against some new, unknown foe. When she got back to the living room she found her mother gazing anxiously down from the balcony at the deserted beach, where the last of the kite sellers was packing up his wares, ready to call it a day.

Peggy looked at the clock. It was nearly six, more than two hours after the time Tobey usually arrived home from school. Jacinta had removed the flower box from the dining-room table and was busy laying place mats and silver. In a few minutes Mr. Jamison would be home.

"I can't imagine—"

"Do you suppose—"

Peggy and her mother spoke simultaneously, and at that very moment Jacinta, more alert than either of them to a sound in the hall, crossed the room and opened the door.

Tobey stood there, small and composed, his schoolbooks carried neatly under one arm. "Hi, Jacinta," he said pleasantly.

Pushing back the hair from her forehead in an unconscious gesture of relief, Mrs. Jamison left her post by the window and asked her son peremptorily, "Where have you been?"

"Out," said Tobey, without any particular emphasis.

"I said, 'Where?'"

"At somebody's house," said Tobey, clutching his

books in front of him and staring at his mother pug-
naciously. Peggy could see that he knew he was in for
a scolding, but he wasn't going to give an inch before
he had to.

"Whose house?" his mother asked.

Tobey didn't move, but he waited a long moment
before replying, and during that time his gaze didn't
leave his mother's eyes. He seemed to be considering
their expression—suspicious, angry, worried, troubled?
—and sizing up the effect of the blow he intended to
deliver. "Ernie's," he said.

Watching in consternation, Peggy saw her brother's
chin rise and jut forward as he spoke, and she knew
that he was making a valiant effort to keep his voice
from trembling. He looked past his mother to the dining room, as though he hoped Jacinta might defend
him, but the maid had gone back to the kitchen. He
was on his own.

"Haven't I told you you're not to play with that
child?" Mrs. Jamison's voice rose to a pitch of fury
out of all proportion to Tobey's crime. "You are going
to be punished, punished severely. And this is an order: you are never to go to that nigra's house again!"

Peggy began to feel desperate. Mother's taking it
out on him, she realized. All the rage she's been building up since we met the Almeidas she's venting on
Tobey! Glancing from her mother to her brother,
standing so alone and forlorn in the hurricane of
wrath sweeping over him, Peggy took a step forward.

She couldn't let him bear the brunt of anger for which he was only the excuse, not the cause.

"Mother!"

"You keep out of this, Margaret!" her mother stormed. "Do you hear me, Tobey? Answer me!"

Tobey stood his ground. In a voice that wasn't very firm, but which was remarkably loud, he said, "Ernie's my friend."

Peggy felt as though her heart were being twisted up out of her throat. Tobey, wounded, was a magnification of herself. She bled for him, and yet she was proud of him, unbelievably proud. Suddenly she ran to her brother and dropped to her knees and hugged him, while his schoolbooks spilled and scattered over the rug. "Baby," she cried, half-sobbing, half-laughing, "baby, you're quite a boy. You've got real guts!"

Utterly astonished, her mouth open, Mrs. Jamison stood and looked down at her children, who were strangers to her at this minute, people she would never learn to know. A key clicked in the lock of the hall door, and she turned, in some passionate hope of escape, to her husband, who came into the apartment wearily, glancing at his embracing children and his distraught wife without really seeing them.

He flung his hat across the room to the sofa, pitched the newspaper he was carrying after it, and rocked back on his heels. "Well," he said, "I guess I'll give you the bad news without beating around the bush. We're being transferred to Salvador, not at the end of the year, but right now. The company's opening a new office there, and they want me to get it going. We've got to pack up and be on our way next week."

Peggy let herself sink helplessly to the floor, too stunned to quite comprehend this new, overwhelming disaster. Tobey's eyes widened in curiosity, and for him the crisis just past receded into limbo. But it was Mrs. Jamison's reaction that was totally unexpected. She sank down on the arm of a chair and started to laugh hysterically.

"Thank God," she murmured, as though it was the answer to a prayer.

Chapter 16

Right now the air was soft. This was the Carioca's city —the bright sea, the lofty mountains, the glittering beaches—but in another two hours the hot metallic sun of noon would sear the pavements, and Rio would be given over to pariah dogs and tourists who ignored the siesta hours.

Having told her mother she must go to Mesbla to buy some buttons, Peggy did her errand and then walked back to the museum along the sun-baked pavement that led from the street toward the vast horseshoe of Guanabara Bay.

She felt drained of feeling, as though last night had taken her beyond the limits of experience to a huge space in which she felt no bigger than Thumbelina. She needed to see Carlos, to tell him all about everything, but in particular the awful truth that they were going to leave Rio, perhaps forever.

"Not forever," he would say.

"Not forever!" she would echo. Oh, Carlos! Peggy began to run.

The side door of the museum was opened by a uniformed guard, considerate, courteous. "Your ticket, *senhorita?*" he asked in Portuguese.

"*Quanto é?*" Peggy fumbled in her wallet for the proper change and walked in blindly, the pictures on the walls mere blobs, the artificial light a mean exchange for the dazzling sun.

"Peggy!"

"Carlos!"

She felt a hand guiding her toward the rear of the gallery, expertly moving her out of the light into the shadow. "Carlos, why—?"

"Don't talk," said Carlos softly. "Just let me look at you."

Peggy stood very still, her eyes big, her throat aching. The white orchid, pinned to the lapel of her suit, trembled like a leaf in a breeze, although the air in the museum was quite still. Her hands, clenching her purse, felt clammy, and she swallowed uncomfortably. Perhaps the urgency of Carlos' message had been a ruse, the rendezvous a clever stratagem. Then how could she ever find words to tell him that she was going away, going away, going away?

The girl and boy were alone in the gallery, which was hung with abstract paintings as anonymous as the attendant who had walked off into the next room. Only Carlos, in this quiet world within a world, was vigorous and alive. Peggy could feel his presence as excitingly as though she were touching him. Everything about him seemed precious to her this morning, the light film of dust on his shoes, the habit he had of holding his head slightly to one side, the freshly laundered smell of his white shirt. He reached out and lifted Peggy's chin with a hand that was gentle but firm, and she was forced to meet his eyes, which were full of affection, but darkly troubled.

"What is it?" Peggy asked, suddenly frightened. "I don't understand—"

Carlos took a deep breath. "Ah, Peggy. I had to see you." He looked down at her, compassionate, confused. "You remember what I've told you—so many times!—that I'm not free."

Not free, Peggy thought. What about me? I'm being torn from everything I love, I'm being dragged away from here. But she couldn't speak. Carlos was too impetuous, too full of himself, too commanding.

"I don't know how to tell you," he said, facing Peggy toward a painting, which was no more than a series of concentric circles on a steel-blue ground. He held her shoulders tightly with one arm, crushing her against him. "I don't know how to tell you, but I've tried."

"Tried what?" asked Peggy thinly.

"Tried to tell you that in Brazil it's different. Peggy, I adore you. I've never known a girl like you. But—"

Peggy waited, pulled together, ready for anything.

Carlos seemed almost to gulp for air. "I'm trying to explain," he said, "about Cleo."

Peggy stiffened. "What about Cleo?"

"Well, you see, we've known each other forever, and it's always been sort of understood—"

Giving him no quarter, Peggy repeated, "Understood?"

"That we'd marry, of course," said Carlos heavily. "She's sort of a cousin. We're very old friends."

"And—?"

"Oh, Peggy, *please* understand. It's Mother, partly. But I've given Cleo my class pin. If she's wearing it, Monday—"

Peggy's eyes widened until they felt as if they would split. Then, without a word, she turned and walked away.

She walked blindly, tear-blurred, past the ticket-seller, past the doorman, past the rank of taxi drivers, past the converging path to the museum's front entrance. She walked across a grass plot, across a boulevard, across a square, around a little blue church, and then she faced automatically toward the suburbs and got on a bus.

She rode past the city, past the apartment, past Copacabana Beach. When the bus stopped she got off.

Freedom, she thought. Freedom.

She walked across the *avenida,* across the sand studded with Saturday's brown bodies, down to the tide line. There she took off the white orchid that was pinned to her gray linen suit, put it down gently, just above the mark of the last wave, and jabbed the corsage pin through the center of the flower. Then she kicked off her pumps, picked them up, and started to walk the two miles back home.

It was a long walk, but the wavelets lapped around Peggy's feet, giving her time to become numb, time to become dry-eyed and able to go through the motions of facing the future.

Free, he had said. "You're free." Well, now she could prove it. American girls—*North* American girls, who weren't coddled by a set of circumstances too soft to be believable—needed an extra something, a sort of built-in courage. Free?

Ooh, she had been a fool! Guida had tried to explain, Becky had tried to warn her, even her own mother had tried to steer her off these bitter shoals. But now she had struck them full on, battering herself to pieces against the jagged ledge of reality. Cleo, pinned. Cleo, triumphant, as she had always implied she would be in the end.

Tears spilled from Peggy's eyes, and she brushed them away and trudged on. The creamy scalloped surf crept across her toes without comfort. Cleo, as good as engaged.

And the villa in the hills, the carriage house in Cambridge. Peggy choked on the thought. She hated Cleo, hated Carlos!

No, no, no! She could never hate Carlos!

His face swam like a mirage before her—laughing, tender, serious, alive with each change of mood. Carlos skimming in to the beach on his surfboard, Carlos lying on the rocks at Gavea, reaching out to touch her hair. It had been born on the beach and it was being buried on the beach, this romance she had thought would last forever. Nothing, Peggy thought, nothing ever again will be quite this shattering. If I can get through this I can get through anything.

The Cariocas were kind. They glanced at the girl, crying unrestrainedly now as she walked along, barefoot, in her town clothes. But then they quickly looked away, respecting her need for privacy in this all-too-public place. They were delighted with happiness, but grief did not come as a surprise.

To Peggy the people on the beach were less than shadows. She walked alone, trying to bring her mind into some sort of focus, so that she could click a shutter on her emotions. Free—is anyone ever free?

Carlos admitted that he wasn't, that he would always be guided by the family, that big and complicated Brazilian institution, whose workings Peggy had barely glimpsed.

But "you're free," he had said. Meaning that she was from the States, where the family did not command. Yet, in a way, it did, because here was Tobey, forbidden the freedom to play with a child he loved, here was her mother, communicating—no matter how wildly and obliquely—her horror at a color freedom, which Brazil cherished but which she feared.

There were so many different kinds of freedom—Dona Virgilia's freedom from the slavery her mother had endured, Tobey's freedom from prejudice, her own freedom of choice, because Peggy knew that when she came of age and wanted to marry she would be her own mistress. Not like Carlos, dominated and obedient.

Yet it never occurred to Peggy to try to persuade him that his submission was wrong. The family was too strong to fight, the Brazilian boy's behavior too rooted in tradition. But such a different tradition from the tradition of the South. Poor Carlos. Poor Mother. Both yoked to the past.

Peggy took a deep, tremulous breath, brought up the damp handkerchief clutched in her hand, and made a tentative swipe at her nose. It was strange to link her mother and Carlos, even for a moment. Yet compared to either of them, she *was* free, and this realization gave her some ray of hope.

If she could just keep putting one foot in front of the other and get through this day!

Despair swept her again and dragged her under, but the tidal wave of grief was over. Now Peggy began to feel ashamed that she was weeping in public. She ducked her head, so that her hair would swing over her cheeks, and hoped people wouldn't notice. She got out her compact and patted the skin under her swollen eyes with powder. How could she face her family in this condition? How could she brave the boulevard, the elevator, Jacinta's tenderness, Tobey's surprise?

As for confronting her parents—the thought made Peggy shudder. There was a word for what she was enduring—not a pretty word. Laurette would say she had been jilted. Pride began to give her the courage to keep her secret, no matter what excuse she made for her tears.

In her heart Peggy didn't blame Carlos. He was just as dear to her today as he had been yesterday. There would never be anyone like him for her, never again. Grownups were wrong to make light of first love. This feeling she had was tremendous, and it would last a a lifetime. There was no use trying to persuade herself that she might someday forget.

And there was no use hoping that the family would be out somewhere when she reached home. They were all on hand to greet her, to be shocked by her tear-swollen face. Her father asked in quick sympathy, "Why Peggy, what's the matter?" and she struggled vainly for a reply, dissolving in tears again, wracked and speechless.

It was her mother who rescued her. "Why, child," she said gently, in real distress, "I had no idea that leaving Rio would mean so much—"

All that day and the next Carlos was never mentioned. If Tobey wondered why the orchid had disappeared, he didn't ask, nor did Peggy's parents. If it seemed strange that she stayed in her room most of the week end, pretending to sort things out for packing, nobody tried to persuade her to do otherwise. She was given the only real sympathy possible; she was left alone.

To go to school was like walking through no man's land into enemy territory, but she managed. She kept her head high and her eyes dry, but at what cost only she knew.

It was not from Guida or from Cleo, but from Becky, that Carlos discovered Mr. Jamison had been transferred to Bahia, but when he tried to accost Peggy in the hall she brushed past him. He caught her arm, twisted her around, started to tell her how sorry—

"Please, Carlos. Please!" she quavered, but it was his eyes, not hers, that filled with tears.

The days passed. Peggy said good-by to Becky and promised to keep in touch. Only as she walked out to the waiting airplane did she break down. She looked back on Rio, wonderful, glamorous, sunlit, neon-lit, starlit Rio, as though she were leaving a whole life behind.

"Seat belt fastened, Miss?" The English came as a shock, a counterpoint to disaster.

"*Sim,*" Peggy said, and the hot tears, held in check during the entire school week, rolled once more down her firm young cheeks.

"Darling, don't be so sad. We'll come back," her mother promised.

"But it will never be the same," said Tobey from the companion seat.

Peggy shook her head in assent. No, it would never be the same. She looked at her brother's childish profile and wished they were more nearly of an age, so that they could talk together. Yesterday afternoon, her bags packed and locked, her closet door standing open on emptiness, she had walked to the window of her bedroom and looked down on the beach.

It was after five o'clock, and the Cariocas had left, carting their grass mats and their umbrellas back to their ocean-front apartments or taking themselves off to their tar-paper shacks in the hills. Only one small boy was down near the tide line, scuffing at the sand and looking anxiously back toward the building-lined, cavernous street, which led abruptly to a mountain five blocks away.

The child bent, straightened, and flicked a pebble out over the waves with a characteristic gesture. Tobey. He sat down, let a wave lap over his buttocks, and stood again, looking not at the ocean, but back toward town.

Then suddenly his whole expression changed. The lines of his body crisped into action, and he ran to meet another child who was skipping across the beach. The two boys stood an arm's length apart, then started down together toward the water.

But the flag is down! It's too late for swimming, Peggy thought.

It was quickly clear, however, that the boys didn't plan to swim. They raced along the high-water mark like puppies, weaving in and out, chasing one another, and although no sound carried to the window above the roar of the sea, Peggy realized that they were yelling at the top of their lungs.

They played for perhaps ten minutes. Then Tobey glanced toward the apartment and Ernie, quickly perceptive, stopped running and came back to where Tobey waited, his body slumped again, the crispness gone.

Peggy watched while the children talked for a moment—she wondered about what—and saw them turn and come up together as far as the serpentine walk. Then, facing one another once more, they shook hands in a gesture which was so tender, so expressive, that Peggy caught her breath. They were saying good-by as surely as she had said good-by to Carlos that day in the museum, but because they were two boys, and not a boy and a girl, their farewell had dignity.

As the pilot turned into the runway Peggy thought, if I had it to do over again, I'd try to be as brave as Tobey. If I could say good-by to Carlos now I wouldn't run away, I wouldn't let jealousy tie me into knots. I'd hold out my hands and wish him happiness. Because I do. I truly, truly do. Oh, Carlos!

The plane taxied along the runway—faster, faster! Peggy tensed, waiting for it to be air-borne. She glanced at her parents, leaning close together, and at Tobey, cracking a wad of bubble gum and sorting through an envelope of travel literature from the seat pocket. Then, turning to the window, she realized that already the buildings below were no bigger than toys, the beach a foot-long crescent of ivory, the mountains flung on the landscape like purple prunes. Now the plane was climbing in a wide arc above the off-shore islands, swinging toward a city that was only a name— Salvador da Bahia—in a distant state, on another uncharted bay.

Peggy took out her handkerchief and blew her nose, trying to face the unpredictable future, hoping that someday soon she would find courage to look back on Carlos with the tenderness Tobey had shown for Ernesto on the beach.

Carlos! The name was less a cry than an echo of a time gone by, a sad but ineffably wonderful time of awakening.

BETTY CAVANNA grew up in Haddonfield, New Jersey, and was graduated from Douglass College, where she majored in journalism. After an editorial job on a Bayonne newspaper, she worked for the Westminster Press in Philadelphia, taking charge of all the advertising. Later, as art director, she bought illustrations for advertising and for periodicals, among them papers for children and young people. It was while reading the stories in these periodicals that Miss Cavanna became interested in writing stories herself, and in 1943 she became a full-time writer of books for young people. She holds an honorary membership in Phi Beta Kappa for her outstanding contribution to the field of juvenile literature. In private life, Miss Cavanna is Mrs. George Russell Harrison. She and her husband live in Belmont, Massachusetts.